"I wouldn't touch you with a barge pole!"

Kendra added, "I've had a lifetime of firsthand knowledge of prospectors already, and that's certainly been enough for me."

"You're strong willed, with set ideas, sweetheart," Rogan drawled, his lips tilting. "You should relax more. You take life far too seriously."

Who was he to criticize *her* attitudes? "Better than taking it too lightly, as you and my brother do."

"You really are difficult to convince that Darby and I are not as alike as you care to imagine." A deeply tanned hand suddenly captured her chin. "Perhaps this will convince you."

Rogan drew her to him and claimed her lips. Kendra felt shaken as a never-before-experienced warmth spread through her.

"Convinced now?" Rogan drawled. "You evidently don't hate prospectors as much as you profess to."

Kerry Allyne developed wanderlust after emigrating with her family from England to Australia, exploring the far horizons of her new country. A long working holiday enabled her to travel the world before returning to Australia where she met her engineer husband-to-be. After marriage and the birth of two children, the family headed north to Summerland, a popular surfing resort, where they run a small cattle farm and an electrical contracting business. Kerry Allyne's travel experience adds much to the novels she spends her days writing—when, that is, she's not doing company accounts or herding cattle!

Books by Kerry Allyne

HARLEQUIN ROMANCE
2527—SPRING FEVER
2593—SOMEWHERE TO CALL HOME
2647—TIME TO FORGET
2725—MERRINGANNEE BLUFF
2737—RETURN TO WALLABY CREEK
2761—STRANGER IN TOWN

HARLEQUIN PRESENTS
361—BINDABURRA OUTSTATION
513—CORAL CAY
743—LEGALLY BOUND
783—TROPICAL EDEN

These books may be available at your local bookseller.

Don't miss any of our special offers. Write to us at the following address for information on our newest releases.

Harlequin Reader Service
901 Fuhrmann Blvd., P.O. Box 1397, Buffalo, NY 14240
Canadian address: P.O. Box 2800, Postal Station A,
5170 Yonge St., Willowdale, Ont. M2N 6J3

Stranger in Town

Kerry Allyne

Harlequin Books

TORONTO • NEW YORK • LONDON
AMSTERDAM • PARIS • SYDNEY • HAMBURG
STOCKHOLM • ATHENS • TOKYO • MILAN

Original hardcover edition published in 1985
by Mills & Boon Limited

ISBN 0-373-02761-3

Harlequin Romance first edition May 1986

CHAPTER ONE

THE early summer night was warm, and as a result of all the windows and doors of the house accordingly being wide open, Kendra Onslow had no difficulty in hearing her brother's approach along the wide and sparsely habited thoroughfare that was the main street of the old mining town of Goldfield in the north of the Australian State of Queensland. The fact that she could also detect another male voice along with her brother's meant that Darby had invited one of his mates home with him from the pub, Kendra supposed, and already in something of an annoyed frame of mind due to the lateness of her brother's return, she made her way out on to the dimly lit verandah with swift, impatient steps in order to form a somewhat less than happy reception committee of one.

Darby and his companion, who appeared to be supporting her brother as much as simply accompanying him, she noted with an even more vexed pursing of her wide and curving lips, had stopped for some reason outside the Onslows' produce store next door—Darby gesturing towards it indeterminately—but with the light behind her it was impossible for Kendra to discern just which of his friends was with him, and so she was forced to wait with arms folded and a foot tapping for them to finally weave their way through the front gate and up to the steps leading on to the verandah before taking them both to task.

On their reaching the steps, however, twin creases of a frown formed momentarily between Kendra's thickly lashed, dark blue eyes on finding that the broad-shouldered man of a couple of inches more than six feet who her less powerfully built brother was leaning against was a complete stranger to her—strangers being something they usually saw very few of in Goldfield—and not one of Darby's normal drinking partners after all.

Not that she allowed that circumstance to sway her from her purpose. After sparing the newcomer only a faint glance to briefly record the strongly masculine face visible beneath the wide-brimmed hat that was sitting at a slightly rakish angle on his self-assuredly held head, the sculptured firmness of his jaw, the fine moulding of his nicely shaped mouth, and a pair of ebony framed, lazily warm grey-green eyes which she found vaguely disconcerting, she returned her stormy gaze to her brother and launched into admonishing speech.

'So you finally managed to make it home, did you? And only four hours later than promised, too!' Her eyes widened sarcastically.

At thirty-two, and older than his sister by nine years, Darby Onslow was possessed of an easy-going nature that made him liked by one and all, and simultaneously made it possible for him to respond to such strictures with nothing more than a cajoling smile—as now.

'I'm sorry, love, but it is Friday night,' he excused in a disarming voice as he began stumbling rather than walking up the steps, despite the aid of his companion who didn't seem quite so worse for wear. 'Besides, we don't want to create a bad impresh ... impression by quarrelling in front of Rogan,' indicating with something of a roll of his head the man mounting the steps with him, 'on his first night here, do we?'

First night here! Just what was that supposed to imply? Kendra frowned dubiously.

'I—I mean, we got talking and time just seemed to get away from us, thash . . . that's all,' concluded Darby with another engaging grin.

'Including the time we were supposed to be at the meeting to discuss the new roofing for the old School of Mines apparently!' she retorted tartly.

'Oh, hell, I forgot all about that!' He did at least look a little abashed now. 'But you could have gone without me. You didn't have to miss the meeting just because I did.'

'I didn't,' he was informed shortly. 'As it so happens, I only got back about half an hour ago . . . to find *you* still hadn't returned!'

'Yes—well . . .' Darby gave a sheepish smile and turned to the man with him to half laugh ruefully, 'I told you she was a real little fire-eater, didn't I?' Adding, after receiving an amused nod of assent in response which had Kendra's temper flaring, 'But since you're going to be here for a while—that is, if you haven't now changed your mind,' with an expressive glance that only succeeded in raising his sister's ire even further, 'I guess I'd better introduce you before we go inside . . . or I forget.' The afterthought was delivered with a wry chuckle prior to his attending to the amenities with little ceremony as he advised, 'My sister, Kendra . . . Rogan Faulkner.'

Doffing his hat to reveal short, coal black hair, Rogan inclined his head deeply—exaggeratedly, Kendra thought—in acknowledgement, but she merely gave a sharp bob of her own in return before swinging her gaze back to her brother.

'I'll thank you to keep your drunken observations regarding my supposed character to yourself, Darby Onslow!' she instructed. 'Or is that all you can think to do while wasting your time in that pub?'

'Uh-uh, not wasting my time . . . as you'll soon

discover.' He wagged a finger at her irrepressibly.
'And nor am I drunk either. Just a little merry, that's
all.'

'That's debatable,' she quipped drily, as always
unable to sustain her exasperation with him for any
length of time, and gave him a gentle push in the
direction of the doorway.

Taking the hint, he began heading somewhat
unsteadily inside, ushering Rogan along with him
down the hall and into the large kitchen at the back of
the rambling old house. Kendra followed them
thoughtfully, her rounded forehead furrowing as she
mulled over her brother's remarks, and no sooner had
the two men seated themselves at the old-fashioned,
heavy wooden table than she brought the matter up.

'Just what did you mean . . . "since he's going to be
here for a while"?' she queried on a suspicious note
with a quick look at Rogan before concentrating her
increasingly askance gaze on her lighter haired
relative.

'Ah, yes, well I told you you were wrong in thinking
I'd been wasting my time this evening, didn't I?
Because after we got talking I found Rogan's done
some mining, too. So as he's a fellow prospector, as it
were, I offered him work here and he accepted,' he
disclosed in triumphant accents.

'Oh, great!' Kendra gibed, her eyes rolling skywards.
'That's all we need . . . another down-and-out gold-
seeker around!' That was all Darby was ever interested
in doing. Digging around on his mining claim for the
reef of gold he was convinced was there. She cast a
meaningful glance in Rogan's direction. 'Another
down-and-out gold-seeker who also likes his grog,
apparently!'

Her condemnation had Rogan sending a com-
municative glance towards her brother in turn. 'You

didn't mention she was also a fire-eating wowser,' he drawled lazily.

'I am not a wowser!' Kendra immediately denied hotly without giving Darby an opportunity to reply. 'I've no objections to anyone drinking ... in moderation!'

'In that case, you've no worries, have you?' returned Rogan somewhat mockingly. 'Or do I look drunk?'

Knowing he didn't, and remembering her own previous thoughts on the subject had Kendra shrugging deprecatingly. 'I—well ... Darby certainly does!' she burst out defensively.

'But then, I'm not Darby, am I?' Ironic smoky-green eyes connected with discomfited blue.

'Besides, I didn't hire Rogan to help me at the mine, but you in the store,' put in her brother on a conciliatory note.

'Me?' She swung to stare at him blankly.

'Well, you are always saying you're left to do everything on your own, and that you dislike having to call Mike down to give you a hand with some of the heavier stuff.' He flicked an eloquent grin towards the man seated at the side of the table. 'Not that Mike ever seems to object, mind you. I think he's rather keen on our little fire-eater.'

Twin spots of colour invaded Kendra's peach-toned cheeks and she glared balefully at her brother for having been so free with his comments, her embarrassment only heightened by the expressive slanting of their visitor's mouth in response to the remark.

'Whether he objects or not isn't the point, Darby!' she flared. '*You're* the one who should be helping in the store!' Pausing, she drew in a calming breath. 'Anyway, we can't afford to employ someone. Goldfield isn't exactly the flourishing town it was eighty-odd years ago, remember.' A touch of sarcasm began edging into her voice.

Before the turn of the century the town had boasted a population nearing twenty thousand instead of the less than one hundred it supported now; the main street had been filled with a variety of thriving businesses, including something like sixty hotels, rather than the meagre few that remained; and there had been numerous producing gold mines, together with their associated mills for separating the precious ore from the quartz and rock it was embedded in. Whereas today there wasn't a single mine still working, only a few prospectors like her brother, picking over the area in the hope of finding something that those who had gone before may have missed.

'At the same time, it's not completely a ghost town either,' Darby obviously felt obliged to remind. 'Granted, it may have shrunk considerably and all the mines closed, but now there's a load of farmers and graziers in the district instead of miners, most of whom prefer to come here for their requirements rather than drive all the way to Red Gap for them.' A journey of some one hundred and forty miles, seventy miles of which were on dirt before they reached the main highway. 'And because of that,' he continued, 'plus the fact that this year has been such a good one for the pastoral industry, what with the good rains we had earlier and all, I reckon we *can* afford to employ someone at the moment because the store's doing better now than it has done for quite some time . . . as you very well know.'

Kendra compressed her lips in a disgruntled grimace. Truthfully, she couldn't dispute his last statement, the store *was* doing better than it had for many a long day, and she did need help, but at the same time she wasn't at all sure it was someone like

Rogan Faulkner that she wanted working alongside her. There was something she was gradually becoming aware of about him, an aura of undisguised masculinity, a physical presence she was suddenly finding oddly disturbing, but which for some vague reason seemed to make it imperative that she try anything she could to have her brother reconsider his decision.

'So despite the fact that I run the store, I'm still not considered sufficiently important to have a say in who should be employed to run it with me, is that it?' she put forward first in not altogether assumed indignation.

'Yes, well, even though I'm sure you'd prefer to have Mike Warden around all the time, I doubt his father could spare him from their own place,' Darby replied in amused tones.

His sister didn't appreciate his humour in the slightest, and especially not since she wasn't particularly interested in Mike Warden in that fashion. Oh, he was nice enough company and a pleasant partner for those entertainments that did take place in the district, but that was as far as their friendship went for Kendra.

'Then perhaps that's just as well because I wasn't even considering Mike!' She refuted his suggestion fierily. 'Not that he's looking for other work, anyhow.'

'But as Rogan evidently is, and we're not exactly inundated with people looking for employment in Goldfield . . .'

He had her there, Kendra had no choice but to concede, even if with extreme reluctance. Offhand, she couldn't think of anyone else they might have been able to employ. For the most part Goldfield's population was an ageing one, the majority of its younger members who hadn't found work in the area already having left for Red Gap and other larger and hopefully more promising centres. With a vexed sigh, she eyed Rogan sardonically.

'Nevertheless, you do know something about stock fodder, etcetera, I trust? The difference between hay, chaff, bran, lucerne, for instance?' Not that she really held out much hope of him not knowing. After all, dressed as he was in faded denim shirt and jeans, short-sided riding boots, and with his obviously well-utilised bush hat that was now resting on the table, he looked more like a stockman than anything else.

'Implying that your customers wouldn't, if I inadvertently selected the wrong ones, presumably,' he proposed on a dry note—but without actually answering, she noted.

'No, that isn't what I was implying at all!' As he was damned well aware! 'I was simply trying to discover how much you know—if anything—about the supplies that are sold in a produce store. Or don't you ever believe in giving a direct answer to a question?'

Rogan rocked his chair on to its back legs, his heavily muscled arms visible below his rolled shirt sleeves folded across his wide chest, a dark brow peaking above goading eyes. 'Well, I guess that really depends on just how I'm asked,' he drawled explicitly.

Once again Kendra felt her face colouring, knowing she had been less than polite when in actual fact the situation was all of her brother's making and she should have been reserving her displeasure for him.

'I'm sorry,' she apologised quietly, if a little stiffly. 'So do you know anything about farm and stock supplies?'

'I figure,' he nodded, an indolent grin catching at the corners of his mouth that had Kendra drawing in an involuntary breath. He really was startlingly handsome, she allowed grudgingly, but for some unknown reason he also made her feel distinctly flustered and to cover her discomfiture she swung away to take some mugs from a cupboard as he continued. 'I've knocked about the bush for most of my life, both on and off properties, so I'd say I'd have as good a knowledge as most when it comes to things agricultural.'

Just as she'd suspected, half-grimaced Kendra in resignation, nodding, but didn't reply as she went about pouring boiling water from the kettle that was always kept ready on the fuel stove on to the coffee she had just spooned into the mugs.

Placing both sugar and milk on the table she then followed with the filled mugs, commenting drily when she deposited her brother's before him, 'You look as if you could use it.'

Darby gave a rueful laugh and fixed her with a coaxing hazel gaze. 'I reckon I could use some food too. I haven't eaten since lunch and I'm ravenous. I don't suppose . . .' He left the sentence implicitly unfinished.

'Don't I always?' Kendra countered wryly and, coming to the decision on impulse that the best way to overcome the unaccountable effect Rogan Faulkner's presence seemed to have disconcertingly had on her would be to treat him no differently than her brother, turned in his direction to propose in the same ironic vein, 'And you're as hungry as he is, no doubt.'

'You wouldn't be wrong,' he owned with another slow smile that did little to help her maintain her composure.

'It would be no more than you deserve if I left you both to starve,' she muttered in direful tones as she moved towards the fridge. She wouldn't, of course, as Darby well knew, but she figured it didn't hurt to at least threaten to every once in a while.'

'I'll give you a hand if it will help,' came the sudden

unexpected offer from Rogan. 'I know my way around a kitchen.'

'Do you?' she was surprised into exclaiming. She hadn't thought him the type. Then she found herself adding the seemingly compulsive question, 'Why, isn't your wife a very good cook?' Since he was of much the same age as her brother she guessed it was more than likely he would be married despite his wife apparently not having accompanied him to Goldfield. They could have been waiting to see if he got work before she joined him, Kendra decided with a queerly flat feeling at the thought.

'Uh-uh, I don't have a wife.' An amused laugh issued from the the deeply tanned column of Rogan's throat. 'I picked up most of what I know about cooking from having been dragged as a kid from one camp to another out in the scrub by my old man in his search for gold, then later while working on cattle and sheep stations. When you're away from the homestead for days and more at a time you have to learn to do for yourself otherwise you go hungry.'

Taking steak and eggs over to the stove, those being the simplest and quickest to prepare, Kendra found herself curious in spite of not wanting to be. 'Your mother didn't object to such a nomadic life?'

His lips twisted crookedly. 'She may not have done, I wouldn't know. Unfortunately she died when I was five after being bitten by a snake. We had a place up around the Adelaide River in the Territory in those days.'

'I'm sorry,' she said sincerely. Then, partly eyeing him with questioningly raised brows even as she reached for the frying pan hanging above the stove, 'And is that where you came from now, the Northern Territory?'

'Mmm, only these days it's Alice Springs that's his headquarters,' inserted Darby informatively.

'In view of my father's likelihood to take off in just about any direction throughout the country on his prospecting searches, we figured that was the most central location to make home base,' added Rogan with a grin.

'I see,' Kendra acknowledged thoughtfully as she dropped the two large steaks on to the grilling plate and added a little oil to the frying pan in readiness for the eggs when their time came. 'Although he didn't come with you to Goldfield, evidently.'

'No, Rogan was saying he's rather occupied up in the Gulf Country at the moment.' It was Darby who answered first again.

'With more gold prospecting?'

'Something like that,' Rogan replied for himself this time, if a little vaguely.

A slight frown creased Kendra's forehead. 'But you chose to come to this district instead,' she mused rather than enquired.

Rogan took a cigarette from the packet in his shirt pocket and lit it before advising with a shrug, 'I was up there for a while, but since I'd never been to this area before, I thought I may as well look it over while I was in north Queensland.'

'It's still a long way to come merely to look a place over, though, isn't it?' she probed on a slightly suspicious note as she turned the steaks.

'Just what are you getting at?' Darby entered the conversation again with a frown.

'I'm simply wondering just what he came looking for, that's all. Work . . . or gold!' The last was uttered with something of a derisive snap.

'So who cares?' he countered, looking somewhat taken aback. 'It's not against the law to look for the latter, is it? Besides, I thought we'd just settled that Rogan will be working in the store.'

Uncertain herself as to why she should care what reason had brought their visitor to the town, Kendra hunched a slender shoulder in a partly defensive, partly defeated movement and began breaking the eggs into the pan. 'I—I just like to know where everyone stands, that's all,' she murmured lamely.

'Then allow me to assure you that I only intend working in the store while I'm in Goldfield.' Rogan's deep voice suddenly sounded so close behind her that it made her start, and on swinging round she found him to be calmly retrieving cutlery from the cupboard drawer nearby as well as salt, pepper, and sauce from the shelf above, which he then placed on the table. Catching her eye, he went on evenly, 'Oh, I'll be interested in having a look at the old mines and so forth, naturally enough, but you can take my word for it, I won't be doing any prospecting.' Abruptly, strong white teeth flashed and a mocking brow lifted as he reached out to tap her beneath her small pointed chin with a long forefinger. 'Satisfied?'

Confused by the unfamiliar sensations his brief touch aroused, she spun back to face the stove rapidly. 'You don't have to explain your intentions to me,' she contended jerkily, not to mention a touch contrarily in view of her previously voiced grievance. 'Or make promises you can't keep.' Her voice began to strengthen. 'You forget, I know what confirmed gold-seekers are like. They can't help themselves! A trace of some colour, no matter how small, and they immediately drop everything else in their quest to discover more. That's how he is,' nodding towards Darby, 'and our father was too, before the mine killed him in a rock fall. And considering the amount of prospecting you've evidently done over the years I've no reason to suppose you're any different.' Pausing, she gave an impatient sigh. 'And for what? A lifetime wasted digging in the dirt for something that isn't even there in any quantity any more!' Taking two plates from the rack above the stove she began lifting the food on to them with unnecessary vigour.

'And that's where we differ,' explained Darby to Rogan with a whimsical grin after their meals had been set before them on the table. 'Because I, as do a lot of others, strongly believe that most goldfields were actually far from worked out in the old days.'

'A theory my old man and I also support,' advised Rogan.

Casting them both an exasperated glance, Kendra removed a loaf of bread from the fridge—the only place to keep it fresh in the heat—and removing its plastic covering began slicing it rigorously.

'And one which we've had some proof of in this district about a year or so ago when one of the local kids found a nugget worth two thousand dollars only a short distance from one of the old mines,' Darby continued. And, with a significant look in his sister's direction when she deposited the cut bread and a dish of butter in front of them, 'There was certainly gold in that in quantity all right.'

'Although I wouldn't recommend you hold your breath until a similar find occurs!' Kendra promptly quipped mockingly, unable to restrain herself. 'That was purely and simply a freak discovery . . . not an indication of payable ore!'

'That party of geologists who've been doing tests on and off for the last six months or more out on the old Southern Cross Consolidated Mine lease may not agree with you,' he was quick to retort. 'They've been very hush-hush about their findings.'

'No doubt because it's all been a fizzer and they've found nothing to talk about!'

'Uh-uh,' Darby disagreed laconically. 'I tend to think it's more likely to be the reverse.'

'Well, of course you would! You're just looking for excuses to corroborate your own baseless suppositions!'

'Baseless?' he repeated in sardonic overtones. 'There's been at least three gold mining areas that have been brought back into production—very profitable production, I might add—in the last few years, just that I know of. So we're,' waving a hand between Rogan and himself, 'obviously not the only ones who believe there's more than a little gold still left in the old workings, and with the more advanced mining and extraction techniques available today . . .'

'None of which you can afford to employ!' she wasn't averse to pointing out.

'Yes, well . . .' He pulled a comically rueful face. 'Until I strike that elusive reef I'm convinced is there, I shall just have to continue as I am, shan't I?'

Now it was Kendra who grimaced, tauntingly, as she started for the doorway. 'Non-existent reef, you mean! Anyway, I'll go and make up the bed in the spare room now, so the two of you will be able to indulge in your futile daydreams to your hearts' content while I'm gone.' She slipped out of the room before either of them could reply.

When she returned some fifteen minutes later after having put fresh sheets on the bed in the room next to her brother's and given the furniture therein a quick dust, it was to find Rogan at the sink doing the washing-up and Darby wielding a tea towel.

'Thank you.' She acknowledged their efforts with appreciation. And to Rogan as she refilled the kettle and replaced it on the stove before damping down the controls for the night, 'You are domesticated, aren't you?'

'It becomes a habit after you've had to make do for yourself out in the bush for a while,' he shrugged casually.

She nodded, watching his competent, economic movements and wryly wishing her brother was as thorough. Darby was all right with a tea towel, but when it came to actually washing the plates the only way she could describe his methods was as decidedly rough.

'Oh, yes,' she suddenly recalled. 'I left a towel and a face cloth on your bed—Darby can show you where the bathroom is—but I'm afraid I couldn't provide any pyjamas,' since he didn't appear to have any gear with him, 'because Darby doesn't use them.'

'That's okay, neither do I,' Rogan half turned to advise drily. 'But I'll collect my stuff in the morning. It's still in the Land Cruiser up at the pub.'

'Mmm, we figured that as young Eddie Hoskings,' one of their two local representatives of the law, 'was just pulling up outside as we left, it could be more prudent for us to walk home rather than drive,' explained Darby with a smile.

'Well, at least it's pleasing to know you still had that much of your wits about you,' bantered his sister, replacing the last of the cutlery in the drawer. 'But now, it's late, and I'm off to bed, so I'll see you both in the morning.' Almost to the door, it was Rogan's voice that had her halting and turning about again.

'By the way, the store opens on a Saturday, I presume,' he sounded.

'Yes, although only until midday.' She nodded. 'It's usually our busiest morning, actually, because that's when a lot of graziers and their families from outlying properties come in to do their shopping, but even if they don't get to the store before closing they all know they can usually find me here afterwards.' She paused, feeling obliged to add, 'But you don't have to start work tomorrow, if that's what you're thinking. Since I wasn't expecting any help, Monday will be soon enough. I'm sure Darby will be only too pleased to take you round town and introduce you to everyone in the meantime.'

'Still don't think I can handle it, huh?' His grey-green eyes shaded mockingly.

Truthfully, that hadn't been the reason at all, but if that was the construction he chose to put on it . . . 'All right, then if you're so anxious to prove you can, start tomorrow by all means.' Halting momentarily, she then went on with an almost gleeful smile, 'We open at seven-thirty on Saturdays.'

'I'll be there,' Rogan drawled, a scanning gaze surveying her suddenly vivacious features in lazy contemplation, while beside him Darby let loose with a burst of laughter.

'You walked right into that one, mate,' he chuckled. 'Take a word of advice from one who knows . . . she's an expert at catching you on the wrong foot, and when you're least expecting it.'

An oblique slant tilted Rogan's shapely mouth, although his gaze remained fixed on Kendra. 'So I'm beginning to realise,' he conceded softly.

'Yes, well, if you've quite finished your discussion of me,' she interposed sardonically, her smile starting to waver and her pulse to behave oddly as a result of such a prolonged and intent scrutiny, 'I'm for bed. Good night.' She took her leave gratefully.

'Night, love. See you tomorrow,' she heard Darby call after her.

'Bright and early,' was Rogan's addition made on a chaffing note that incomprehensibly had her heart abruptly beating faster.

Think of, and treat him just as another brother,

Kendra found herself repeating continuously as she made ready for bed a short time later. That way he wouldn't be able to have such an unaccountable effect on her, she reasoned. Not that she could satisfactorily explain why she should have reacted to his presence as she had to date, anyway, especially when he was only another quixotic prospector, after all. A reminder she found vaguely disappointing, much to her irritation, but which she ejected from her mind determinedly as she thereafter forced her thoughts to remain steadfastly fixed on other, less disturbing matters until she eventually drifted off to sleep.

CHAPTER TWO

IN the morning Kendra washed and dressed quickly in her normal attire of jeans and shirt before making her bed and hurrying out to the kitchen where she discovered her brother in the process of pouring himself a cup of strong, black coffee.

'Feeling the effects of last night, are you?' she enquired wryly as she bustled about stoking up the fire in the stove, adding wood to it from the box alongside, and then taking sausages, eggs, bacon and tomatoes from the fridge.

'A little,' admitted Darby sheepishly, resting his head gingerly on one upraised hand while lifting his mug to his lips with the other.

'Serve yourself right. It's self-inflicted,' she censured, but with a fond smile, and tossed him a headache powder which he accepted appreciatively. 'So where's the Territorian? Still out of it?'

'Hell, no.' He went to shake his head but decided against it. 'He was just leaving to collect his transport as I wandered out here. He should be back any minute. God, he must have a hard head ... and a strong stomach,' he mused in rather envious tones. 'He looked as bright as if he'd never touched a drop of the stuff, and yet he had beer for beer with me last night.' He paused briefly while easing himself carefully round on his chair in order to look at her more closely. 'So what do you think of him?'

'He's okay, I guess,' she shrugged, mindful of her decision to think of him as nothing more than a duplicate of her brother. Then flashing a sudden grin, 'For a useless, impractical prospector, that is.'

'Oh, yes, that's right, attack while I'm in no condition to offer any defence,' groaned Darby eloquently.

'And whose fault is that, dare I ask?'

'Huh!' He made an expressive grimace. 'Unsympathetic brat! I've a good mind to . . .'

Just what he intended was never voiced as Rogan's return diverted him, and from then until breakfast was concluded the conversation turned to other matters.

'So what do you have on your agenda for today?' Kendra asked of him, however, as she and Rogan were preparing to depart for the store. 'I don't suppose you feel like fixing the back fence? If it gets much worse we'll have those cattle in the vegetable garden before too long.'

'Sorry, not today, love,' Darby advised regretfully. 'I more or less promised Vivian I'd go down there this morning—she's apparently having trouble with her drains, or water pipes, or something—and then this afternoon I thought I'd take Rogan round to meet a few of the blokes. So he doesn't feel quite so much the stranger in town, as it were.'

So all of her brother's drinking mates could welcome another to their midst more likely! surmised his sister sardonically and sighed. 'Okay,' she acknowledged on a resigned note. 'But keep it in mind for the future, won't you? It really doesn't look as if it will last much longer.'

'Will do,' he acceded cheerfully. 'Will do.'

And with that she guessed she would have to be content, thought Kendra with a rueful twist to her soft lips, and began leading the way across to the store.

Keeping pace beside her, Rogan eyed her thoughtfully for a moment before querying laconically, 'Vivian?'

'Vivian Blackwood,' she elucidated. 'She's the

widow of Darby's best friend who died a few years back. Craig and he grew up together, went away to the same boarding school together, and even for a time worked Darby's mine, the Good Cheer, together. So naturally when Craig and Vivian married, Darby was their most frequent visitor and, after Craig's death, he just seemed to consider it was his responsibility to do all he could to help her, and her young son, Jimmy, in any way he could.'

'She doesn't have any family of her own here in town?'

Kendra shook her head. 'No, they all live in Red Gap. Where Vivian herself came from originally.'

'Wouldn't it be easier for her if she returned there to live, then?'

'Probably, I suppose.' She shrugged. 'But since she's never mentioned wanting to do so, I guess she just prefers it here. Although it may not appear much of a town to some, those of us who live here like it just as it is.' A somewhat defensive note made an appearance in her voice as she unbolted the side door to the store and led the way into its cavernous interior.

'Don't get touchy,' chipped Rogan with a half laugh, following her inside. 'If I didn't prefer bush towns myself, I wouldn't still be living in the outback either.' So saying, he turned his attention to the massive proportions of the building interestedly.

Constructed towards the end of the last century during Goldfield's boom years the store had, naturally, been built to serve a considerably larger population than it did at present, and although now inevitably showing signs of its age in places, it was still possible to see the dedicated workmanship that had gone into its making, especially in the typically ornate woodwork that decorated every conceivable vantage point and the large, multi-paned arched windows.

'At a guess, I'd say it wasn't built as a produce agency initially,' he suddenly looked down to contend.

Having been unconsciously studying him while he surveyed the store, Kendra flushed at having been discovered doing any such thing and averted her gaze swiftly. 'No, my great-grandfather had it designed originally for a general emporium,' she conceded in something of a rush. Adding meaningfully in an attempt to regain her lost composure, 'He was one of the smarter ones, for although he actually came looking for gold he soon realised there was more likelihood of his being successful selling goods to the miners than by taking his chances mining. It was when the gold began to peter out just after the turn of the century and people started leaving the town and district en masse—the outcome being that the top end of the street bacame the main shopping area—that his son, my grandfather, decided it would probably be more advantageous to turn it into a produce store.'

'Which you've been running ... since when?' he enquired as she moved away to open the front doors.

'Since my mother died when I was fifteen.' She shrugged, returning now and making for the much larger doors at the back.

Rogan watched her retreating figure meditatively. 'Meaning, your mother was in charge of it before you?'

Kendra finished swinging the doors wide before answering. When she did, it was in noticeably caustic tones. '*Someone* had to be if we wanted to eat regularly! Certainly neither my father nor Darby, as you may have already guessed, ever showed any interest in it.' She broke off, a mirthless laugh springing to her lips. 'Which might have been quite humorous really, if it wasn't so ludicrous!'

'What makes you say that?'

'Oh, just the fact that the males in the family who were around when the gold *was* still here didn't want anything to do with mining it, while the two who should have known there wasn't any ore left became obsessed with looking for the stuff!'

Rogan flexed a broad shoulder dispassionately. 'From talk at the pub yesterday, I gather there's a number of people in town who believe there's still more gold in the ground here than was ever taken out of it.'

'Yeah, yeah, I know. The reef all the old-timers were positive extended eastwards from the Jubilee Mine and which the Orion Deeps and the Southern Cross Consolidated No 2 shaft were supposed to intersect . . . but never did!' she added pointedly. 'Why do you think my father took out a claim for the Good Cheer where he did? Because he believed those old rumours, too, and that's why it's right along the same line as the Deeps and the Consolidated No 2, of course!' Pausing, she heaved an ironic breath. 'Not that it did him much good for all he, or Darby, ever took out of it.'

'Although I was told they both have had *some* finds.'

She nodded. 'Not that you'd have wanted to try and live on the proceeds from them, however,' she half laughed with grim humour. 'As you must know, having been involved in the same thing yourself.'

His acknowledging grin was wry. 'It certainly has its ups and downs all right,' he conceded.

Having abruptly found herself more than a little fascinated by that indolent shaping of his attractive mouth, Kendra drew a vexed breath and hastily looked away. 'Yes—well—and now to business,' she said briskly, trusting the change of subject would preclude any further such lapses in her attention. 'As you can see, most of the stock feed is kept at the rear of the store—it's easier for loading that way. We don't have any bales of lucerne at the moment, but if anyone asks for it you can tell them we expect to receive another supply some time next week.' She took a few steps to one side of the building. 'Over here we have the chemicals—dips, drenches, and the like—and in that corner,' pointing towards the front, 'veterinary supplies, as well as saddlery and a variety of horse bits, bridles, shoes, and so on. This side,' walking in the other direction now, 'is where the fertilisers, cattle licks, dog food, chook food, calf supplements, molasses, are stored. While in the shed out the back there's all the fencing and chicken wire, steel stakes, sheets of iron, and so forth.' She looked about her cursorily. 'There's also a number of other items I haven't mentioned, of course, but no doubt you'll come across those as time progresses.'

'Such as the honey down there?' Rogan indicated a jar-laden table set just inside the front door.

'Mmm, we sell that on Vivian's behalf, actually. She keeps bees and sells the honey as a supplement to her income as a casual teacher's aide at the local primary school. From time to time she also brings in some bananas and pawpaws for us to sell, too. There's not so much of a market for those, of course, because mostly everyone grows their own fruit and vegetables, but the honey's a good seller. It's very nice.'

'Some of which it looks as if she's about to sell.' He smiled on seeing a tall, slim woman, accompanied by two young children, enter the store and immediately pick up a jar before continuing further inside.

'Mmm, that's Gwen Edgar, the butcher's wife. She's a real fan for it.' Halting, she cast him a questioning glance. 'So shall I serve her, or do you want to have a go?'

'Got to start some time,' he drawled lazily and without more ado started off in the woman's direction.

'Oh, by the way, the price lists for everything are pinned on the wall behind the cash register over there,' Kendra called after him, gesturing towards a small counter midway along one wall.

Rogan merely glanced back over his shoulder, nodded his comprehension, and continued on his way.

Despite being ostensibly occupied doing something else, Kendra watched him surreptitiously, noting the air of self-assurance and command she speculated would always allow him to take and maintain control over any situation, the movements that exuded an innate strength and grace, the engaging quality of his ready smile and easy manner—and the effect they were obviously having on the not normally particularly talkative Gwen Edgar! Why, she was positively chattering away to him as if he was a long-lost friend instead of a complete stranger, she suddenly realised, her wide mouth pulling into ironic lines.

But as the morning progressed, it soon became evident that it wasn't only their female customers who became more expansive in his presence, because the men did as well, Kendra noted. Only in their case it appeared to be due not merely to an apparent acceptance of him as their equal in knowledge of rural matters, but also, and perhaps more significantly, as a result of their seemingly immediate recognition of him as a man's man. A judgment Kendra couldn't dispute, especially when she was of the same mind, and the more so since she suspected that to have also been the very reason he had found such ready approval in her own brother's eyes.

Nevertheless—not that she had really needed any confirmation, anyway—the morning's trading also proved beyond a doubt that he was definitely a woman's man too. In consequence, it really came as no surprise to her when Genevieve Searle—some three

years older than Kendra and the daughter of one of
the town's two publicans, as well as being something
of the local *femme fatale*—came wandering into the
store shortly before closing time. She saw the dainty
redhead's dark brown eyes light up with interest as
soon as they alighted on Rogan's indisputably good-
looking features and powerfully built form.

'Is there something I can do for you, Genevieve?'
asked Kendra drily as the other girl drew abreast of
her, wondering just what had brought her to that end
of town that particular morning of all times. It was a
very rare occurrence for Genevieve to visit the store.

With evident reluctance, the redhead swung her
gaze from Rogan, who was presently occupied with a
customer, to concentrate on Kendra instead. 'For a
start, you can introduce me to *him*,' she half laughed
expressively, and quite open in her interest. 'I heard
yesterday that Darby had employed some stranger—
some impressive hunk of a stranger, according to Joy
Landers,' she inserted with another eloquent bubble
of laughter, 'to help out in the store, but knowing Joy,'
the barmaid at Darby's favourite watering hole, 'that
could have meant anything. However, on this occasion
I'm glad to say she's right. He *is* something, isn't he?'

Refusing to be drawn into agreeing with her—for
preference she would rather not have discussed Rogan
at all—Kendra hunched a slender shoulder in studied
indifference. 'He's just another unsuccessful, down-
and-out prospector as far as I'm concerned,' she
declared in repressive tones.

'Oh?' Genevieve's brows arched high in astonishment, the eyes beneath them beginning to register
amusement. 'Not that I can say I altogether blame you
of course, under the circumstances, but you've never
had any time for them, have you? But then, perhaps
it's just as well in this instance, because no matter

what *he*,' eyeing the subject of their conversation avidly, 'does for a living, it won't be deterring me from going after him, and I wouldn't like to think I was maybe causing you some distress by sweeping him off from under your nose, so to speak.' She smiled with dubious concern.

Not much you wouldn't! grimaced Kendra inwardly, acidly, having seen the redhead do the same to others without a qualm before. Aloud, she merely murmured with a hint of sarcasm, 'How very thoughtful of you.'

'Yes, well, you know how it is in a town the size of Goldfield.' Genevieve sighed, obviously taking the sentiment at face value, and totally oblivious to any satiric inflection. 'You do have to take others into consideration all the time.'

'Including Rex?' Kendra was unable to resist quizzing. As far as she was aware Genevieve and Rex Thorley, the son of a local grazier, were supposedly on the point of becoming engaged!

'Rex?' the other girl repeated somewhat absently, as if the name wasn't all that familiar to her. Then, on apparently realising how she must have sounded, gave a laugh and excused airily, 'Oh, well, he *is* away at present—for a couple of months, in fact—and he *did* tell me not to allow his absence to curtail my activities.'

How unbelievably trusting of him! thought Kendra wryly. Surely he was aware of his prospective fiancée's reputation for having a somewhat fickle nature. She shrugged. Not that it was any concern of hers, in any event.

'Then while you're waiting to—umm—generate some activity, is there something I can serve you with?' she enquired, lightly ironic.

'Actually, I only came to check out the town's newcomer,' Genevieve disclosed candidly. 'Although I don't really suppose I should make it that obvious, so maybe you had better get me something.' She looked about the store quickly. 'One of those bags of dog food will do. We always seem to be running out of that.'

Kendra's mouth twitched in irrepressible amusement at her choice. 'Do you think you'll be able to carry it?' They only stocked the large sizes and she knew from experience just how much they weighed.

Something Genevieve only just appeared to realise as, on glancing at the item again, she frowned in disappointment. 'Well, you could always deliver it, couldn't you?' she proposed. A brief pause, and her expression altered to one of delighted triumph. 'Or better still, since it is almost time for you to close, if I asked very nicely perhaps your new assistant would be so gallant as to carry it home for me.' She sent a pleased gaze towards the back of the store. 'What's his name, anyway?'

'Rogan. Rogan Faulkner,' Kendra supplied crisply. 'While as for the other, I don't really think it's right that you should expect . . .'

'Oh, don't be such a killjoy, Kendra!' Genevieve interjected to brush her objections aside loftily. 'It's up to him to decide, not you. You just get the bag and let me take care of the rest.'

Sighing, and wondering why she cared if the other girl inveigled Rogan into doing as she wanted, Kendra lifted an indifferent shoulder and went to do as suggested. In the act of pulling a bag from the pile a call behind her had her stopping and looking up.

'See you, Kendra!' Rogan's last customer sent her a friendly wave before departing via the back doors where his utility waited, loaded with stock feed and fertiliser.

'Yes, see you, Norm!' She smiled back and, surmising from the empty street outside that he had probably been their last customer for the morning, left what she was doing for the moment in order to go and shut and bolt the front doors.

While doing so, the sound of Genevieve's laughter—warm, husky, coquettish—drifted across to her, arousing feelings of inexplicable irritability as, on returning to the pile of dog food, she saw that the older girl was already engaged in sparkling conversation with Rogan.

'Here! I'll carry that for you,' he offered, taking a step towards Kendra on seeing her begin dragging the bag to the counter.

'No, thanks, I can manage. I always have before,' she asserted in a snappish show of independence. And on finally reaching them, 'I gather you've already introduced yourselves, have you?'

'Obviously.' It was Genevieve who answered with something of a smirk, although the look in her flashing brown eyes indicated she was none too happy at the interruption.

Purposely ignoring the hint to make herself scarce, Kendra moved to the other side of the counter. 'Cash or account?' She glanced at the redhead enquiringly.

'Account, naturally!' came the terse advice. Followed by, for Rogan's benefit, a flirtatiously tittered, 'You'd think she would know by now. After all, our family has only been dealing here for the last fifty years or more.'

'And sometimes your father chooses to pay cash,' retorted Kendra with an explicit smile of her own as she started to make out an invoice. When it was completed she handed it across to Genevieve, asking innocently, 'Would you like it delivered, or have you—er—made other arrangements?'

Almost snatching the slip of paper from her, the other girl then proceeded to aim a coy glance in

Rogan's direction. 'Well, as a matter of fact,' she began in a sweetly helpless tone, 'I was wondering if you might be so very kind as to help me home with it. I'm afraid I'm not used to heaving such weights around, whereas I'm sure it would present no trouble at all to your magnificently developed muscles. And it is required urgently.' Issued as a wheedling extra.

Unable to listen to any more, Kendra cut in sardonically before Rogan could reply. 'If you'll excuse me, I think I'll go and close the back doors.' Before I throw up! she added expressively to herself as she quickly took her leave.

The task completed, she turned back to see Rogan hefting the bag of dog food effortlessly on to a broad shoulder and, with a contentedly smiling Genevieve beside him, begin heading for the small side opening.

'You'd better not be long,' she recommended curtly. 'Lunch will be in about half an hour.'

'Oh, but you'll lunch with us, won't you?' Genevieve immediately turned pleading eyes upwards. 'It's the least we can do when you've been so obliging.'

Rogan smiled down at her lazily, and brought an involuntary glower to the younger girl's face as a result. 'There's really no . . .'

'But I insist!' Genevieve broke in on him with a playful half laugh. 'You don't have to bother with it, Kendra. It's all settled.'

With a slight flexing of his unladen shoulder as if in submission, Rogan still slanted a brow-raised glance in Kendra's direction—much to her surpise—but which she was suddenly in no mood to respect. 'It's nothing to do with me,' she contended in deliberately squashing tones. 'Your time's your own once the store's closed.'

Briefly, his thickly framed, grey-green eyes continued to hold hers regardless, and then Genevieve catching at his arm distracted him.

'You see, it is all settled!' she exclaimed happily. 'In any case, you shouldn't let Kendra's sharp tongue put you off. She's always been like that, and you'll simply have to learn to ignore it as the rest of us do.' With a faintly malicious look towards that girl before she slipped through the side doorway.

Feeling the heat of discomfiture warming her smooth cheeks, and reluctant to see Rogan's reaction to the remark—was that really how everyone thought of her, as being sharp tongued?—Kendra promptly made for the counter where the cash register was situated in order to hide her mortification, and was relieved to discover that she was alone when next she glanced up.

By the time Darby put in an appearance for his lunch, Kendra had already eaten hers. Or as much of it as she could manage, her appetite seeming to have abruptly deserted her.

'Where's Rogan? Had his already, too, has he?' queried her brother as he tucked in to cold meat and salad.

Seated opposite him, her hands cupped around the mug of tea she had just poured herself from the pot on the table, Kendra shrugged offhandedly. 'I wouldn't know. He went off with Genevieve for lunch at her place.'

'Went off *with* . . . or was carted off *by*?' Darby half laughed on a drily graphic note.

'I didn't see him exactly fighting to escape her.' She grimaced.

'No? Well, maybe he would have made more of an effort if you weren't quite so intent on giving him such a hard time.' A whimsical grin touched the edges of his mouth.

'If I weren't . . .!' She spluttered to a halt. 'I've treated him no differently than I do you!' Well, mostly she had, she qualified to herself.

'Mmm, but then I know you only half mean a lot of what you say about prospecting and prospectors . . . he doesn't.'

Kendra's smoothly arched brows lifted to a sarcastic peak. 'So what are you suggesting? That I throw myself at him like Genevieve did this morning?'

'You could do worse.'

'What!' She stared at him aghast.

'Well, I like him.' He shrugged, continuing with his meal, and appearing completely unperturbed by her stunned reaction. 'And I think you probably would, too, if you could just overcome your prejudice against him for a while because of his interest in gold mining. I mean to say, it's not even as if he intends to do any while he's here, and the fact that he took up my offer to work in the store proves he's got no objections to turning his hand to something else.'

'No doubt because even prospectors like to eat occasionally,' she was quick to mock. 'Besides, as I have no intention of chasing after any man—even one you apparently get on with so well—nor of altering my opinions . . . not prejudices,' she corrected meaningfully, 'then I guess, if he can't take it, he'll just have to continue consoling himself with Genevieve, won't he?'

'You could be right,' he acceded more casually than she expected. Pausing, he raised a pair of wryly twinkling eyes to hers. 'Provided, of course, you're prepared to reap what you sow.'

'Meaning?'

'Only that Rogan Faulkner somehow just doesn't give the impression he's used to being bested, so I still wouldn't be inclined to ride him too hard, if I were you, love,' he recommended on a dry note.

'Is that right?' She returned his gaze challengingly. 'You don't consider my sharp tongue,' using the expression deliberately, satirically, 'capable enough of protecting me?'

'Uh-uh!' Darby shook his head slowly, but unhesitatingly. 'Not that your description is one I would've used, anyway, but you forget I happen to know that there exists a much softer, and very caring nature, beneath that fire-eating image of yours.' He smiled at her affectionately. 'So just take it easy, huh?'

'For my own sake?' She smiled back, although with still a hint of defiance in her tone.

'Something like that.'

'We'll see,' was as much as she was thoughtfully prepared to concede. Then, on a brighter note, 'So how did you go at Vivian's? Did you manage to fix what needed repairing?'

'Partly.' He nodded. 'I told her I'd finish the rest tomorrow. I needed to come back for a new section of water pipe and an elbow, anyway. That was the main trouble, hers have rusted through.' Leaning across to the bench beside the sink he pushed his now empty plate on to its laminated surface. 'And Rogan? How did he make out in the store?'

'Okay.' She shrugged. But almost immediately stricken by a sense of guilt for not giving credit where it was really due, promptly amended, 'No, surprisingly well, actually. He hardly needed to refer to me for anything.'

'I thought that's how it might be,' Darby averred. 'From what he was saying last night, he appears to have worked at just about everything in the bush at one time or another.'

'Such as?' Kendra was astounded to suddenly find herself asking.

'Oh, stock work of just about every kind, post-cutting, fencing, droving, well-sinking, shearing, even catching snakes for serum laboratories, and birds for southern zoos. You name it, and he seems to have done it,' he laughed.

'Hmm . . .' Annoyed for even being interested, she reverted to her original topic rapidly. 'And Vivian? How was she this morning?'

'Oh, good.' Hesitating momentarily, he went on to muse, 'She's such a kind and softly spoken girl—or woman, I suppose I should say, since she has an eight-year-old son.' Darby gave a wry half laugh. 'She's always so grateful for anything you do for her. She never fails to keep me supplied with cups of tea and things to eat while I'm working there.'

'Mmm, Vivian's like that. She's lovely,' Kendra was only too willing to agree. 'She won't say a bad word about anyone if she can say a good one instead. It's such a shame she lost Craig as she did.'

'Yes—well . . .' Darby released a heavy breath and began rising to his feet. 'Now I guess I'd best be on my way to collect Rogan. I said I'd take him round to meet some of the fellers this afternoon.'

'Providing he's still of the same mind now that he has Genevieve only too willing to keep him company,' she suggested in distinctly sardonic tones.

Darby came to a halt with his hand on the flyscreen door. 'Hmm . . . That could be a possibility, I suppose.' Abruptly his mouth shaped with humour. 'On the other hand, of course, he could also be anxiously awaiting my arrival. Genevieve can become somewhat—er—exhausting after a while.'

'I doubt he's noticed,' Kendra gibed.

He merely laughed and continued out through the door. 'I'll see you,' he called back from the verandah.

'But not as late as last night!' she promptly crossed to the doorway herself to instruct.

'I promise.'

'You always do!' his sister answered wryly. 'Besides, there's a movie on over at the hall tonight that Mike and I were planning to see.'

'That's right, so there is. Vivian was saying she was thinking of going, too,' he recalled. 'Okay, I'll make certain we're not late for you.'

'You'd better!' she mock-growled as he bounded lightly down the steps to the ground below, and received a broad grin in response before he disappeared from view.

Quickly disposing of the small amount of washing up, Kendra then turned her attention to collecting any dirty clothes that hadn't yet been consigned to the laundry underneath the elevated house, including those she retrieved from Rogan's room after only a moment's indecision as to whether he would appreciate her searching through his belongings. An uncertainty she overcame by telling herself that, due to his absence, there was no choice if he wanted clean clothing. With the washing machine loaded and swishing away energetically, her next task was to prepare a leg of prime lamb and vegetables for their dinner that night, after which she grabbed a hat from behind the kitchen door and headed for the back yard.

Tending to the brilliantly flowering shrubs, fruit trees, and vegetables therein she had always found to be a relaxing as well as rewarding pastime rather than a chore, even though the area covered almost three acres, and in between hanging out a couple of loads of washing she spent the remainder of the afternoon happily weeding and digging, pulling out old plants and replacing them with new, as well as picking ripe fruit and vegetables. Those they didn't eat she could always preserve.

Engrossed in what she was doing, she was quite

unaware of the passing of time until she heard Rogan and Darby's voices approaching, whereupon she looked up with a start to realise just how long the afternoon shadows were.

'Oh, don't tell me it's that late!' she gasped as they neared her, scrambling upright from her kneeling position and brushing roughly at the blades of grass and particles of dirt that were adhering to the legs of her jeans.

'No, as a matter of fact we're early,' advised her brother reassuringly.

'That's a relief!' She wiped the back of her arm over her perspiration-damp forehead in an expressive gesture and then bent to recover the tools she had been using. On rising again, she slanted him a bantering glance from under long, curling lashes. 'How come? Did someone run out of beer?'

'Ungrateful wench, isn't she?' Darby grinned ruefully at Rogan before turning back to Kendra to impart, 'No, as it so happens, it was solely for your benefit—in an effort to make up for last night.'

'In that case, I thank you.' She swept off her hat in a flourishing salute. But as they all started for the house, it was to Rogan that her eyes waywardly strayed and she just couldn't restrain from quizzing mockingly, 'You did manage to tear yourself away from Genevieve in order to do the rounds with Darby, then?'

'I kept a prior arrangement I'd made, if that's what you mean,' he returned with equal goading.

Kendra dropped her gaze, grimacing. So he hadn't found the other girl's company as wearing as Darby had predicted he might, she deduced, feeling strangely depressed.

'And only until this evening, when he'll apparently be escorting her to the movies,' relayed Darby, whimsically informative.

All of a sudden Kendra found her own interest in the evening's entertainment waning considerably, but rather than show it made herself eye Rogan again in a baiting manner. The same as she would have done if such news had related to her brother.

'My, my, the pair of you must have had a gratifying lunch,' she quipped.

'Mmm, there was certainly no conflict,' he was quick to advise expressively.

Meaning, like there was with herself, she surmised, and gave her dark curls a slightly defiant toss as a result. If he didn't like it he could always move into the hotel where, doubtlessly, Genevieve would be only too happy to laud his every word and action.

'That must have been encouraging for you,' she sniped bittersweetly and, spinning on her heel, veered towards the laundry in order to wash her soil-stained hands before taking in the washing.

With a partly wry, partly retaliatory narrowing of his gaze in response, Rogan merely continued on with Darby up the steps and into the house, where Kendra discovered him in the kitchen a short time later on carrying in a basket of dry clothes. Of Darby there was no sign, the sound of running water emanating from the bathroom informing her that he was probably taking a shower.

'There's some of your things here, too,' she immediately announced, albeit on a somewhat diffident note, as she deposited the basket on the table. 'I hope you had no objections to my going into your room to collect them.'

'None at all,' Rogan owned, his mouth shaping crookedly. 'Although I wasn't expecting you to do my washing for me.'

'I didn't, the machine did,' she dismissed facetiously. 'But since you only have the one small bag of gear with you I thought it more than probable you'd have some that will need doing regularly.' Pausing, she couldn't suppress the sardonic words that rose involuntarily to her lips next. 'Particularly if you're planning to indulge in a hectic social life while you're in town.'

'Hectic?' He raised an explicit brow. 'A night at the movies?'

'Plus an—er—obviously enthralling lunch, of course. And that's only on your first day in town!'

'You object?'

'Not at all,' she rushed to disclaim. 'As I said this morning, it's your choice as to what you do outside of store hours. It's certainly nothing to do with me how, or with whom, you care to spend your time.' And in an effort to add weight to her deliberately snubbing statement, turned her attention to the clothes basket to eventually bring forth a few articles that belonged to him. 'If you want any of this for tonight I'll iron them for you.' The offer was briskly voiced.

Rogan indicated a pale lemon, silk knit shirt, then went on to veto with a shake of his head. 'You don't have to iron it, though. *That* I can do for myself.' He made to extract it from among the rest.

'I doubt it,' Kendra promptly scoffed, whipping the shirt out of his reach before he could touch it. 'If you're anything like Darby with an iron it will have more creases in it when you've finished than it had before you started.' She turned for the cupboard where the ironing board was kept with the garment still in her hand.

In an abrupt and entirely unanticipated movement, Rogan wrapped a sinewed arm around her waist from behind as she passed him, sweeping her off her feet effortlessly, and holding her firmly against his rugged

frame while determinedly relieving her of his shirt
with his other hand.

'Except that it's time you realised I'm *not* Darby ...
as I've pointed out previously,' he reminded in
roughening tones prior to setting her to the ground
once more.

Caught offguard by his unexpected action, not to
mention being more than a little disquieted by his
sudden proximity, Kendra's first irrelevant thought
was that he had never spoken a truer word if only for
the fact that she knew only too well her brother would
never have been able to lift, and continue to hold her
suspended, with such obvious ease. Not that her
curving form carried any surplus pounds, but simultaneously, at five foot seven she had never
anticipated being treated as a lightweight either. God,
he must be strong! followed the grudgingly impressed
thought as she rapidly, composingly, put more
distance between them.

'I was merely trying to help,' she retorted in
somewhat accusing accents, attempting to dispel those
feelings of disconcertion that still lingered. 'There was
no need to resort to force to take it from me.'

'Apparently I considered otherwise,' he drawled
uncontritely. 'If only in an effort to stop you from
keep confusing me with your brother.'

'Oh, I don't *confuse* you with him,' Kendra
contradicted, defensively glib. 'I just see the inescapable
similarities, that's all ... whether you would rather
deny their conspicuous existence or not! Because make
no mistake, you are two of a kind, Rogan! Dreamers,
chasing after a pot of gold at the end of every
rainbow—or should I say, end of every mine shaft?—
and wasting your lives in the process!' Halting, and
totally oblivious to the disappointment that had been
evident in her voice, she sighed wearily and gestured

towards a tall cupboard in one corner. 'The iron and the board are in there if you're so determined to use them.' And without waiting for a reply, or even giving him time to make one, she picked up the basket from the table and made her way through to the sewing room where the remainder of the washing could be attended to later.

It was close to dinner time when Kendra finally returned to the kitchen, showered herself now and this time dressed in baggy, burgundy coloured slacks and a white, close fitting, sleeveless jersey top. Busying herself with the last-minute preparations for their meal, she acknowledged both men's presence only briefly when they joined her, although she still couldn't help noticing, and reluctantly conceding, that Rogan had been right in saying he could iron. There wasn't a crease to be seen in the lemon shirt he had teamed with the dark brown pants that fitted his lean hips so trimly. Admitting such to herself was something else again to saying so to him, however, and so she pretended not to have noticed, or to have forgotten, by concentrating on the task at hand and thereby all but ignored both him and her brother until their dinners were actually on the table.

Even then Kendra remained uncustomarily quiet throughout the meal and the hasty washing up that followed, listening only absently to Darby and Rogan's discussion on the various facets of gold mining, her own thoughts bewildered, her feelings confused. She just couldn't understand why Rogan should be capable of disturbing her equanimity in the fashion he had on many occasions, or even if it came to that, why she seemed even less capable of preventing it from happening. After all, it wasn't as if he meant anything to her. How could he when he was simply another footloose miner who, despite being temporarily otherwise employed, was just as likely to up stakes at any moment and disappear into the bush the minute he had sufficient funds to carry on prospecting again?

Unfortunately, this last thought only succeeded in making Kendra feel unaccountably dissatisfied once more—although undoubtedly only due to it being more than obvious that Rogan Faulkner had both the personality and the ability, if he cared to use it, to really make something of his life instead of merely throwing it away on futile pipedreams, she rationalised swiftly—and in consequence when Mike Warden arrived her greeting was much more warmly and effusively voiced than usual.

Mike, at twenty-five, at least had his future mapped out already. He would take over his father's general store in total when the time came, and then he would really set in motion his scheme for not only completely modernising his own family's business premises, but also encouraging and persuading everyone else in town to do likewise in the name of progress.

A plan Kendra this evening forgot she was at odds with—she preferred the character and air of elegance projected by the town's remaining old buildings with their latticed verandahs and lace-scrolled balconies, even if they were a little dilapidated these days—as she watched in some surprise to see Mike's normally confident and controlled demeanour alter to one of hesitation coupled with a definite tinge of antagonism on being introduced to the newcomer in their midst. Of course, the fact that Rogan's greater height immediately appeared to make Mike look, and perhaps feel, at a disadvantage—he only being a couple of inches taller than Kendra herself—may have been a determining factor in his losing some of his self-assurance, she deduced, but it wasn't until they were walking along the street to the old School of Mines building where the movie was to be shown that she realised the reason for his previous display of barely concealed animosity.

'So how long's that Faulkner feller going to be staying with you?' he demanded rather than asked of Kendra in a muttered aside so that Darby, who was accompanying them, couldn't hear. Rogan had already departed to collect Genevieve.

'I wouldn't know,' she shrugged, her voice only a little more audible than his had been, 'but I shouldn't expect it will be for too long. You know how prospectors are,' with a sardonic curving of her mobile lips, 'once it's in their blood nothing can keep them from it very long.'

'Oh, he's one of those, is he? I didn't realise.' Mike's voice noticeably lost some of its tautness, knowing his companion's feelings on the subject. 'Not that I'm in favour of Darby having hired him in the first place, though! I mean to say, with him living there, too, it could just give the bloke ideas with regard to you, couldn't it? He doesn't look the type who'd get many knock-backs from females.'

Why, he's jealous! gaped Kendra in astonishment, and then bit at her lip, frowning. So how to restore his customary better humour by explaining he had no reason to be, but in such a way that he couldn't construe it as inferring he meant more to her than he actually did? With another slight hunching of one shoulder she half smiled at him wryly.

'After today's efforts I rather think Genevieve will be doing all in her power to keep him occupied in that respect while he's here.'

'Well, whether she does or not, I still think Darby had no right inviting him to live with you,' Mike protested sharply. 'It's bad enough him expecting you to look after him all the time while he fritters his days away in that damn stupid mine of his, without adding to your burden. Why doesn't he get a proper job for once, or even just help out in the store, if it comes to that?'

Although it was a criticism she herself had levelled at her brother many times, as far as Kendra was concerned it was solely a family matter and, as always, she conversely took very strong exception to anyone else attempting to fault him. She loved her brother dearly and there wasn't anything she wouldn't have done for him. Even if his chosen way of life did aggravate her at times she still wasn't quite as opposed to it as she implied on occasion, and especially not when to her mind he possessed many other endearing qualities that more than made up for any such supposed shortcomings.

'Darby does not *expect* me to look after him . . . I choose to do so!' she therefore saw fit to contradict, and not a little heatedly. 'And the reason he doesn't get a job is because he's already doing what he likes best! Just as I'm quite happy running the store!'

'Apart from those times when the supply trucks arrive and *I've* had to help with the unloading, presumably! As I remember, you've often had plenty to say about his absence then!'

'Yes—well—that's true, of course,' she had no recourse but to accede. 'And I've always been very grateful for your assistance. None the less, since you never appeared to object to helping . . .'

'Well, naturally I didn't!' he broke in on her forcefully. He caught her to him possessively with an arm around her shoulders, his blue eyes darkening as they sought hers, his voice deepening imperceptibly. 'And you know why, don't you?'

Abruptly faced with just what she wanted to avoid, Kendra drew a dismayed breath and quickly dragged her own gaze away, not knowing quite what to say without hurting his feelings.

'Come on, you two, you're not alone don't forget.
Save all that huddling together for later, huh?' came
the chafing interruption from Darby who was strolling
a couple of paces behind them, and for which his sister
could have hugged him.

'Sorry.' She immediately turned to half laugh in
relief, and surreptitiously easing out from beneath
Mike's arm dropped back in line with him. 'Did you
think we were ignoring you?'

'It was starting to appear that way,' he averred, a
teasing grin catching at his mouth.

In the meantime, and as a result of Kendra's action,
Mike, perforce, had had no option but to follow her
lead and join Darby also, although in his case with
more vexation than gratitude showing on his fairly
formed features.

'Actually, for the most part we were discussing
Rogan Faulkner,' he disclosed in a return to less
tolerant tones. And eyeing the older man intently,
'You're a bit keen inviting him into your home when
you know so little about him, aren't you?'

'Evidently I disagree, or I wouldn't have done so,'
countered Darby nonchalantly. 'Besides, since he was
going to be working in the store . . .' He shrugged
significantly.

'That's all very well, but it wouldn't have made all
that much difference if he'd put up at one of the
hotels, surely?' Mike persisted.

'Except that I happen to consider him a friend . . .
and friends of ours,' nodding to include Kendra,
'don't stay in a hotel while they're in town.'

'A friend!' Mike looked openly scornful. 'How could
he possibly be? By all accounts you only met him the
day before yesterday!'

'So I make friends easily,' Darby quipped with
imperturbable good humour.

If Mike was attempting to get a rise out of her brother as a vent for his own apparent displeasure, then he should have known better, mused Kendra drily, because it was just about impossible to have an argument with someone of Darby's even-tempered and forbearing nature.

'You also have no qualms about making extra work for Kendra just as easily, apparently!' shot back Mike.

At that Darby frowned, although not at his critic, but at his sister, in concern. 'I'm sorry, love. I guess I just didn't think,' he apologised promptly. 'I suppose it has . . .'

'No, it hasn't!' Kendra broke in to deny before he could even finish what he was saying while simultaneously slanting the younger man a furious glare. How dared he interfere in such a manner! 'And since I certainly haven't made any such complaint, there's absolutely no call for you to apologise either!' She paused, her expression taking on an ironic cast. 'In any event, to be quite truthful, I think I'd have to say my work's lessened since Rogan arrived, because now I don't do any of the washing up at all. The two of you do it, whereas before,' with a meaningful glance in Mike's direction, 'I used to share it with you.'

Her refutation had both men's countenances changing. Darby's clearing and relaxing again, Mike's losing most of its disgruntlement on realising he had gone too far and becoming remorseful instead.

'I'm sorry, but I was really only thinking of you,' he contended quietly as they neared their destination.

'Then for that, I thank you,' Kendra acknowledged. And pleased that he seemed to have reverted to his more usual mien, followed it with an expressively smiled, 'But having known me as long as you have, did you honestly believe I wouldn't, or couldn't, speak up for myself if I thought it was warranted ... particularly when prospectors are involved?'

'Hmm ... I guess I should have known better, shouldn't I?' He laughed, linking his arm with hers, and approaching the hall—which was all that was really left of the old School of Mines nowadays—in much higher spirits.

Kendra too felt easier in her mind with his return to a more amiable attitude, and it made her own manner more relaxed as she greeted and talked to those people also just arriving, or still clustered outside the hall. Observing Vivian Blackwood standing alone for the moment, Darby immediately set off in her direction, the pair of them joining Rogan and Genevieve when that couple put in an appearance a few minutes later, Kendra noticed.

'Do you want to sit with them?' enquired Mike on also noting the other four who were now beginning to enter the building.

'Not especially.' Kendra's refusal was rapidly given along with a decisive shake of her head. 'I'd rather sit with Maureen and Jonno, wouldn't you?' Already flashing a bright smile towards the young couple, the female member of the two being clad in a full-fitting maternity outfit, who were even then bearing down on them with the same idea obviously in mind.

'Suits me fine,' endorsed Mike with evident pleasure, and presently the four of them were also making their way into the hall.

Inside, the lights were still ablaze—the showing of the programme dictated by everyone's arrival rather than by any scheduled starting time—and after they'd settled themselves into a row of chairs near the back, Kendra found herself scanning those others present involuntarily. Darby and Rogan, along with their partners, were seated some distance away, she discovered, but try as she would to ignore them her gaze kept swinging in their direction throughout her ensuing conversation with Maureen and her husband until the lights were finally doused.

Irritated by such a lack of concentration—Lord, why should she care or even be interested, if Genevieve had moved her chair as close as possible to Rogan's, or if that girl's whole infatuated, flirtatious performance was an unmistakable invitation to a more intimate relationship?—Kendra now made a determined effort to keep her attention glued to the screen in front of her, and for a while she was successful.

However, as the movie's storyline unfolded, and proved neither as entertaining nor as absorbing as she had anticipated or as she would have wished, once again seemingly ungovernable impulses had her glance wandering, always towards one particular area, much to her disgust, as well as to such an extent that she eventually lost track of the film's story altogether.

This fact made her even more vexed with herself on becoming the subject of some strange looks from her companions when she was able to add so little to their discussion of the plot as they left the hall afterwards, plus downright irate, not to say discomposed, on later finding herself unable to sleep on reaching her bed because she was subconsciously registering the time it took for Rogan to return after taking Genevieve home!

CHAPTER THREE

As Sunday was the only day of the week when Kendra wasn't obliged to rise early, she made the most of her time in bed the following morning. Partly, she had to admit, because she hadn't finally closed her eyes until after two—the time Rogan had eventually made it back to the house. No prizes for guessing what he'd been doing until that hour, she had grimaced with a sort of caustic despondency at the time.

Now, though, as the palate-teasing aroma of cooking bacon began to permeate her room, reminding her of her own increasing hunger, she threw back the sheet and padded down the hall in bare feet to the bathroom for a wash before donning a pair of faded denims and a coral-coloured, stretch singlet top and then heading for the kitchen.

Darby and Rogan were already seated at the table when she entered, each of them doing justice to brimming plates of steak and eggs, and the crisply curling bacon that had prompted her to join them. Shortly, Kendra was doing the same, although in her case, minus the steak.

'You didn't exactly rush home last night ... or—umm—this morning rather, did you?' The sardonically taunting remark slipped out before she could put a brake on it the first time her eyes connected across the table with Rogan's lazy grey-green gaze. There was something in the way he seemed to always look at her—a knowing, teasing mockery perhaps—that compulsively made her want to retaliate somehow.

'You were checking?' he drawled on a provoking

note that merely served to corroborate her previous conjecture, but which this time she did at least manage to disregard in her flurry to deny any such thing.

'No, of course not!' None the less, her face still flamed at the falsity of her disclaimer, and she dropped her discomfited gaze swiftly to her plate before continuing with a supposedly demurring shrug, 'I simply happened to hear you come in, that's all.'

'Well, I sure didn't,' put in Darby blithely as he poured himself a cup of tea. 'I died the minute my head hit the pillow. I might add I was more than a little pleased to reach it, too. I think those drinks we had yesterday afternoon must have caught up with me some time during the evening.'

A corner of Rogan's shapely mouth tilted wryly. 'I know the feeling . . . especially after having been plied with a whole lot more on taking Genevieve back to the hotel.'

For a moment Darby stared at him askance—as did Kendra, even if covertly—and then he started to laugh, uproariously. 'I know what happened to you! Genevieve's old man collared hold of you to inspect that gun collection of his! I should have warned you about him. He does it to everyone given half a chance. You only have to mention the word gun in his hearing and he'll keep you talking on the subject for hours.'

'Don't I know it!' Rogan looked ceilingwards expressively. 'I just happened to admire that old Brown Bess he has over the fireplace and that was it for the next three hours! I had to see every firearm in his collection, not to mention help him dispose of the best part of a bottle of a Napoleon brandy before I was allowed even the smallest chance to take my leave. Genevieve simply gave up trying to divert his attention along other lines after about an hour and went to bed.' He angled an explicitly goading look at

Kendra as he delivered this last piece of information, which promptly had her creamy-skinned cheeks flushing afresh.

So not only had he disproved her assumption, but he had also been well aware just what it had been! she realised in mortification, and took no further part in their continuing conversations as she attempted to recover her self-possession, at least outwardly.

'Oh, before I forget, you've nothing planned for the rest of the morning, love, have you?' It was Darby who addressed her towards the end of the meal in casual tones, and caused her to glance up, albeit a trifle in surprise, at the question.

'Not really,' she owned. 'Why?'

'Because I more or less promised Rogan you'd give him a guided tour of the town—the various old mine and mill sites, that sort of thing,' he divulged with a disarming grin.

Or was it really a sheepish one? questioned Kendra of herself, fixing him with a direful glare. How could he have betrayed her by making such a suggestion when he knew all too well she didn't exactly see their new employee in the same favourable light he evidently did! But now, having been treacherously trapped into confessing she had no particular plans of her own, what possible excuse could she give for getting out of it without making it embarrassingly clear that it was mostly her own illogical reactions to Rogan Faulkner's presence that made her wary of spending much time, especially alone, in his company?

'Oh, but . . . I—I'm sure he'd much prefer you to be his guide,' she parried, sweetly hopeful. 'Why don't you show him round?'

Darby shrugged philosophically. 'I would if I hadn't promised Vivian I'd finish that work for her today.' Pausing, he sent her a smile she could only have called studiously ingenuous. 'Besides, you remember all the interesting little incidences concerning the mines better than I do.'

The brute! Kendra heaved mutely. He had his own excuse down pat! But at the same time it was beginning to appear as if he actually *wanted* her to be Rogan's guide, although for what reason she was at a total loss to fathom. Nevertheless, it was just that suspicion that finally had her submitting to the suggestion.

'Oh, all right . . .' Halting, she suddenly swung her attention to Rogan in a last effort to evade the task. 'Unless, of course, *you* would rather wait until Darby was free to go with you, or—or maybe Genevieve . . .'

'Genevieve!' her brother cut in to repeat in amused disbelief. 'What use would she be? You know very well she can hardly distinguish one mine site from another, let alone provide anyone with any information concerning them.'

'I—well—I just thought Rogan might consider her—umm—company more than sufficient recompense for any lack of knowledge,' she returned with an eloquently chaffing smile in the darker haired man's direction.

'Uh-uh!' Rogan dismissed the idea with an idolent shake of his head. 'As you should be aware, it is knowledge someone connected with the mining game's interested in when they're on a goldfield—old or otherwise. While as for waiting until Darby has the time . . .' He flexed a broad shoulder smoothly. 'I'm quite happy with today's arrangement—and as the saying goes, there is no time like the present, after all.'

More was the pity! gibed Kendra inwardly, and then sighed in resignation. It seemed the die was cast. Had been, in fact, even before she had known the idea was being proposed, by the sound of it! She leant back in her chair, making a rueful moue.

'So what parts do you want to see? Anything in particular?'

'Why, all of it, naturally!' came the insertion from Darby that had her silently promising to have some very definite words with him as soon as she got him alone. ·

'That could take considerably more than one morning—or even a day for that matter!' she turned to fire at him.

'So?' he countered with whimsical humour. 'You're not planning on leaving town, are you?'

She was starting to wish she was! 'Well, whatever we don't get to see today, you can always show Rogan later, can't you?' She put the onus back on to him with a forced but subtle smile.

Darby's own mouth quirked wryly. 'That could be all of it if you don't make a start shortly.' He indicated the now empty plates and cups on the table. 'In the meantime, you can leave all this to me, if you like. I'll do the washing up before going down to Vivian's.'

Oh, he *was* prepared to be helpful in order to pack her off with Rogan! She only wished she knew why! But since he had seen fit to offer her services without first consulting her, she thought it only poetic justice that she accept his latest magnanimous offer— especially knowing he neither liked the chore, nor was really expecting her to take him up on it. Revenge really was sweet at times, when all was said and done.

'Okay,' she assented with purposely cheerful insouciance, rising to her feet. And looking across the table with questioningly raised brows, 'Shall we go?'

Gaining his own feet, Rogan inclined his dark head lazily. 'You lead, and I'll follow, precious,' he drawled.

Momentarily, the unexpected and resonantly voiced soubriquet caught Kendra off balance and had her colouring warmly. Then, recovering, she responded to Darby's comically crestfallen expression with a breezily smiled, 'We'll see you later, then,' before crushing her mass of short curls beneath a round-peaked cap that had been hanging on the back of the kitchen door and moving out on to the verandah.

'Wretch!' charged Rogan on a drily humorous note as he settled his own wide-brimmed headgear into place on descending the steps beside her. 'You know very well he wasn't expecting to be left with that lot to do on his own.'

'He offered.' She shrugged, trying hard to repress a grin. She cast him a taunting look from beneath long, sweeping lashes. 'In any case, I didn't exactly hear you offering to help with it either.'

'Perhaps because I figured that, if I had stopped to assist, you may have contended that too much time had already expired to make any such tour worth-while.'

Now why hadn't she thought of that? 'What, after I'd more or less agreed to show you around?' she half gasped in pseudo innocence.

A hand abruptly catching her by the nape of the neck caused a disturbing, breathless feeling to overtake her and her heart to beat faster. 'Aware as I am of your bias against prospectors, I wouldn't put anything past you, sweetheart,' he mocked.

'All the more reason then for you to have had Genevieve accompany you, maybe. It's more than obvious she doesn't hold any such prejudices,' she retorted, pulling an explicit face as she dragged free of his hold. 'Or were you just at a loose end because, for some hard to imagine reason, she wasn't available today?'

Rogan thrust his hands into the back pockets of his jeans, their steps taking them along the main street now. 'As it so happens, she isn't in town today,' he relayed with a surprising, to Kendra at least, unconcern. 'I understand she'd made prior arrangements, which were impossible to break, to visit one of the local properties.' The Thorleys', no doubt, surmised his listener sardonically. 'Not that it would have made any difference if she had been here, because I would still rather have had you as my guide.'

Fighting to quell the unruly feelings of pleasure that assailed her at his last words—God, she wasn't so adolescent as to be flattered by anything one of his irresponsible breed had to say, was she?—Kendra forced herself to eye him with studied nonchalance. 'Why?' The question came out more baldly than she intended, even so.

'Well, with your record, at least from you I can be reasonably sure of getting the truth, the whole truth, and nothing but the truth,' he disclosed with an expressive laugh. 'I doubt there'll be any fanciful embellishments, grandiose claims, or highly flavoured hearsay.'

'Oh, I see.' She experienced a stupid and vexing sense of disappointment that she couldn't explain but which only a furiously determined effort was able to overcome. 'Right, nothing but the plain, unadorned facts shall you have, then,' she proposed astringently at length. Then swiftly, in the same concise vein, 'So to start at the very beginning, the area was first proclaimed a goldfield—it being Crown land at the time—in 1870 after gold had been discovered just behind where the present school stands, to be precise, by two separate parties of wandering prospectors, their names being . . .'

'Hey!' Rogan clasped hold of her arm and spun her to face him. 'I may have said I was only interested in the truth, but that doesn't mean you have to shoot it at

me as if from a machine gun,' he chided in ironic
tones. 'So how about we start again, and you take it a
little slower and with more expression this time,
hmm?'

Kendra twisted away from him fractiously. 'I
understood that was the only reason you wanted me
here. To regale you with the bare facts.'

'And if I said it wasn't?'

There was a slight alteration in the timbre of his
voice that made her suspect his countering question
may have had a double meaning, and as a result her
pulse jumped erratically for a moment in a nervous
turmoil until she assiduously forced it back under
control. She must be mad to permit him to affect her
so! With a deeply drawn breath she made herself eye
him steadily.

'Then you would be disappointed, because that's *my*
only reason for being here,' she declared on a note
infused with camouflaging firmness.

'In which case, there should be nothing stopping us
from proceeding in full accord, should there?' he
quizzed in a return to his more anticipated provoking
tones.

It made her wonder if it hadn't actually been there
all the time, and berating herself acrimoniously for
having let her imagination run away with her, she
shook her head quickly as she automatically began
heading for the path that led to the top of the highest
of the tailings heaps that abounded both in and around
the town.

'So what *do* you wish to know about Goldfield,
then?' she queried as they made their way upwards.

'For a start, why we're climbing this mound on such
a hot morning,' Rogan's reply came graphically.

It was hot, Kendra had to concede. His reminder
making her wipe the back of her hand across her

temples to remove the dew of perspiration that had already begun to form there. 'Because without making the journey all the way out to Duffey's Peak,' gesticulating towards the apex of the low, rugged and tree-capped range that dominated the otherwise undulating landscape a half a mile or so away, 'it's the best place for viewing the whole of the town, of course.' She half smiled a trifle tauntingly.

Rogan merely contented himself with a speaking glance as they tackled the last part of the climb which became progressively steeper the higher they rose until at last they made it to the crest. Although not without him having had to give Kendra a hand to overcome the final and sharpest incline, much to her chagrin, due to the erosion of the fine particles by the district's seasonal rain at the beginning of the year having destroyed most of the previously utilised footholds.

'It seems it was just as well I was along or you may not have made it,' he wasn't above goading after pulling her up beside him.

That was in retaliation for her previous remark, she supposed, although it still didn't prevent her from promptly retorting, 'And if it wasn't for you, I wouldn't have been here in the first place!'

'Then I've done you quite a favour, haven't I?'

She frowned, not a little warily. 'In what way?'

'Because I suspect anyone who's so unaverse to making the climb up here on such a day must have quite a feeling for the view so gained, and that being the case ...' He hunched a checked cotton clad shoulder meaningfully.

Astonished, not to say somewhat disconcerted, by his unexpected perception, Kendra partly turned away, raising a diffident shoulder of her own as she looked out over the scene below.

'Yes—well—I do like it up here, as it so happens,

even though some would probably call it un-
prepossessing for the most part. In fact, when I was
younger . . .' She came to a sudden halt, unsure why
she had even felt the desire to go on, but most of all
reluctant to allow him any insight into her life or her
feelings. There was no telling what she might
inadvertently reveal, and with that obviously all too
shrewdly discerning trait of his he might also deduce
just how he disturbed her on occasion. To cover
herself, she went on to ask instead, 'So what do you
think of it?'

'Surprisingly rewarding,' he replied on a soft note
that had her swinging back to look at him curiously,
then immediately averting her gaze again in confusion
on finding his ebony lashed eyes to have been intently
surveying herself rather than the view.

'Y-yes, you can see just about everything from up
here,' she stammered, trying desperately to concentrate
the conversation on their reason for being there. 'This
being the largest dump, of course, because the
Invincible crushing mill which operated on this site—
unfortunately only the engine block brickwork and the
concrete slab of the assay room floor remain now——'
pointing them out amidst the tall yellow grass below,
'was the last to close down. That was in late 1914.
Most of the mines had gone by then, too, so when the
remaining men also started to depart in order to join
the army that just seems to have been the final death
knell for Goldfield as a mining community.'

'It's a typical story for most of the old gold towns.'
Rogan nodded, much to her relief that his attention
had evidently reverted to the information she was
imparting. 'Although the name's rather more unusual.
Wasn't the place ever officially called anything else?'

'By all accounts it was supposed to have been,' she
relayed with a half smile, relaxing more as she became

further involved with the subject. 'But apparently there was a long and heated debate—between those two parties I mentioned who made the first discoveries here—over which of them was to have the honour of naming the field once it was proclaimed. Well, they never did agree, and as more and more miners poured on to "the new goldfield" near Saddlebag Creek in the months that followed, it wasn't long before the words "the new" were dispensed with and it became just plain Goldfield—which it's been ever since.'

'I guess it was at least appropriate,' he allowed, the corners of his mouth curling with amusement.

Kendra experienced a quickening inside her in response and continued with her narrative hurriedly. 'Now, over there,' indicating some mullock heaps just past her brother's favourite hotel, the North Australian, 'is where the Morning Star P.C. Mine was situated, while those remains of poppethead legs that are visible just beyond it denote the site of the Homestead Central No 2 Mine. Then we have the Queen Anne, the Camelot, the Diadem P.C., the Great Northern Mill, the Jubilee Extended Mill . . .' She faithfully recounted all the mines and mills as she slowly turned full circle. 'And last, but by no means least, there's the Conqueror Mine, which despite its name, was the field's greatest failure.'

'Its shaft didn't hit pay-dirt?'

'That's something of an understatement!' came the dry retort. 'The total depth was just over two thousand feet, but without a cracker to show for it. The old timers apparently reckoned it was just incredible they didn't hit a reef because there were just so many of them in the vicinity, and the Conqueror certainly wasn't one of the last to be sunk on the field. However, somehow it was managed, as well as to send its syndicate bankrupt, not unnaturally, one of them even committed suicide by throwing himself in the mine's dam.'

'Hmm . . .' Rogan mused ruefully. 'And the field's greatest success?'

'Oh, the Jubilee Extended Mine.' Kendra's reply was given in unequivocal tones. 'It was unbelievably rich and produced over a million pounds' worth— money, that is, of course—of gold. A really fabulous sum in those days.'

'It's not exactly to be sneezed at today either,' commented Rogan whimsically. 'Although, as I understand it, not all of the mines went out of production due to the ore having been fully depleted, even so.'

'No,' she had little option but to grudgingly admit. She had been wondering how long it would be before he raised Darby's, and apparently his, pet theory. 'There were a number that were forced to close because they simply couldn't overcome the problems of having reached the water table, while the Queen Anne and the Southern Cross Consolidated were shut down after an explosion and a fire respectively. However,' her voice gathered strength, 'in most cases it *was* the considerable decrease in the ore that made them uneconomical and so brought about their eventual closures.'

Rogan nodded, watching her amusedly. '*You* don't believe, nevertheless, that the Queen Anne or the Southern Cross Consolidated at least could have prospects in this day and age.' It was more of a statement then a question.

A scoffing grimace was Kendra's initial response. 'Darby's Good Cheer,' flinging out an arm in the general direction of her brother's mine on the far outskirts of town, and the ramshackle structure that housed his single stamper equipment for the necessary crushing and separating, 'isn't all that far from either of them, but I haven't noticed him, or my father before him, exactly discovering a fortune!' She paused slightly before adding with equal feeling, 'Nor, might I add, has Jon Fisher who also mines out that way!'

'Jon Fisher?' he repeated thoughtfully. 'That's the other feller you were with last night, isn't it?'

She was surprised he should have known, but then, presumably Darby had mentioned it for some reason or another, the two of them being in the same game. 'Mmm, his wife, Maureen, and I have been friends ever since I can remember,' she supplied casually. Then, in more pungent tones, 'I think she must have suffered a temporary loss of sanity when she married him, though. A prospector, for heaven's sake! She used to have more sense!'

'Perhaps she simply considers love a more fulfilling substitute,' suggested Rogan mockingly. 'Because she certainly appeared happy enough last night. Moreover, you seemed to be on good terms with him, too, as I recall.'

'Oh, Jonno's nice enough, I'll give him that,' she hurried to assert, not wanting to convey the wrong impression, but at the same time surprised once again to discover that he'd been aware of her reactions the previous evening. She hadn't realised he'd even spared one glance in her direction. More importantly, however, his first taunting comment had aggravated and now she returned his still faintly sardonic look with a gibing one of her own. 'Unfortunately, though, love isn't such a fulfilling substitute for food! So maybe it's just as well Maureen has extremely generous and tolerant parents who are willing to help out in that regard, otherwise she and Jonno really would be in dire straits if they had to rely solely on what he makes from the mine. The same as Darby and I would be, too, if it wasn't for the store!' She released a disgruntled breath. 'It's all very well being starry-eyed over someone, but that isn't the be-all and end-all of life. There are still other considerations to be taken into account ... as Maureen herself once used to agree!'

'In other words, you're just cut up because her thoughts obviously don't align with yours any more!' Rogan charged caustically.

'That's not true!' Kendra promptly flared on a highly indignant note. 'I just think it's a crying shame that she allowed her feelings to rule her head to such an extent that she agreed to marry a gold miner! One thing's for sure, I'm thankful to know the same will never happen to me, because I wouldn't touch one of you with a barge pole! I've had a lifetime of first-hand knowledge of them already so I know what I'm talking about, and that's certainly been enough for me, thanks very much!'

'Happily, there are others who aren't burdened with any such hang-up, however!'

Hang-up! Her blue eyes flashed with a fulminating light. 'Then fortunately for them they've evidently never had a close connection with a prospector, because if they had they'd soon come to realise the mindless futility of it all, wouldn't they?' she sniped. 'And what's more, deflating as it may prove to be for you,' she went on with suspect sympathy, 'I wouldn't put too much store in that assumption either if I were you, because if it's Genevieve you're using as an example ...'

'It wasn't,' he cut her off in dry accents. 'It was Vivian, as a matter of fact.'

'Vivian!' Her exclamation was as incredulous as her expression. 'Whatever are you talking about? You're surely not going to tell me that, on the strength of one meeting, you've managed to infatuate her also!'

Another satiric, and impulsive reference to Genevieve. Which it was obvious he recognised by the manner in which his firmly moulded mouth quirked with ready taunting in retaliation. 'With her being such a charming and unassuming lady,' a description that was meant to imply the complete opposite to herself, Kendra was positive, 'I would have deemed it an honour to have done so, but as it happens I suspect any such feelings of that nature are directed towards someone else entirely where Vivian's concerned.'

'But the only person she ever goes anywhere with . . .' She came to a shocked halt, her eyes widening. 'You mean, Darby?' she gasped. 'Oh, but that's out of the question! They're just good friends, that's all, on account of Darby having known her late husband so well. It—it's preposterous to think it might be anything else.'

'Is it?' He lifted an expressive brow.

'Well, of course it is! For starters, why on earth would she want to take on someone like Darby who, kind and easy-going though he is, not only hasn't a paying job, but very rarely can make it home any evening without first stopping off at the pub for some drinks with his mates beforehand . . . as you can verify! Goodness knows I've tried to break him of the habit long enough.'

'Except that, in such instances, you seem to have overlooked the fact that a wife is likely to have markedly more—shall we say, persuasive power?— than a sister. Particularly when the man in question has evidently proved on a great many occasions already that the lady only has to mention something requiring his attention and he promptly drops everything in order to assist.'

Granted, that was more or less how matters stood,

but ... 'You're now also suggesting Darby's in love with Vivian?' Kendra deduced in disbelief.

Rogan gave an explicit shrug. 'Is it so unlikely?'

'Yes, it is!' She didn't hesitate to dispute. 'He would have said something to me, I know he would, if he really did feel that way about her. And—and if it was the case, why hasn't he asked her to marry him, then? There's nothing to stop them from marrying, if that's what they both want.'

'As to that, perhaps time will be the telling factor.'

'Mmm, the factor that disproves every unbelievable claim you've just made, no doubt!' she derided, despite her inward decision to pay more attention to her brother and Vivian in future. There couldn't possibly be any truth in those claims ... could there? 'Anyway, we seem to have digressed. We're supposed to be discussing the town of yesteryear, not the people in it today.'

'And especially not when those people happen to be close to you, hmm?'

'Meaning?' Her wide-spaced eyes met his challengingly.

'You're a very strong-willed character, with equally set ideas, sweetheart,' he drawled wryly, his lips tilting. 'You should relax more, you know. You take life far too seriously.'

'Better that than taking it too lightly, as Darby ... and you do!' Kendra was quick to gibe in return, spinning on her heel and making for the edge of the mound where the path led downwards. Who was he to criticise *her* attitudes? she fumed.

'There you are again! Getting the two of us confused once more,' Rogan goaded lightly as he caught up to her. A deeply tanned hand suddenly captured her chin, tipping her face up to his. 'You really are difficult to convince that we're not as alike as you care to imagine, aren't you, precious?'

Concerned at the disquieting manner in which her senses were starting to behave at his nearness, Kendra broke away from him restively, and anxious to increase the distance between them further, hastily, if a little ungracefully, half jumped and half slithered down the sharp incline to the less steep path below. From where she felt more able to return his darkly framed, grey-green gaze defiantly.

'Since to date I've yet to see or hear anything that would change my mind, that's hardly surprising, is it?' she retorted on a sarcastic note.

With a speed that startled her somewhat and had her taking an involuntary step backwards, Rogan made it down to her level in an agile and far more controlled fashion. 'Then perhaps this will help separate me from your brother in your mind once and for all,' he declared, drawing her to him swiftly and claiming her soft lips with his own in a determined possession she was helpless to evade.

Indignation had Kendra struggling furiously for release, but clasped tightly as she was against his powerful frame by one arm, her head effectively immobilised by the other, his far greater strength made it an impossible desire to achieve—as she was forced into eventually conceding.

What she wasn't prepared to acknowledge, however, was the way in which her emotions gradually, uncontrollably, began to react to the insistent, relentless demands of his sensuous mouth. A never-before experienced warmth was spreading through her, disturbing in its intensity, and devastating in effect. She felt shaken, her legs weak, and as his searing lips continued to demolish her resistance knew her own to be not only traitorously responding but capriciously parting as well.

Only then did Rogan allow her freedom. 'Convinced

now?' he quizzed indolently on raising his head.

That his breathing should have been as steady as a rock, where she was desperately attempting to calm hers, had Kendra's smooth cheeks burning even more hotly in humiliation than they had at the thought of her wayward response. 'Yes! Of the fact that Darby at least knows how to treat women decently . . . you obviously don't!' she lashed back scathingly.

'While you, my precious, just as evidently don't hate prospectors—well, not everything about them, at least—as much as you profess to,' he wasn't above mocking.

There was no need to ask what had prompted that remark, but in spite of the embarrassment that made her want to avoid his all too-knowing gaze, Kendra tenaciously refused to permit him to discompose her any more than he had done already.

'Except that I never did say I hated them . . . just that I found them rather pitiful, that's all!' she disparaged in dulcet tones.

To her irritation he merely grinned imperturbably. 'You sure didn't display any such pity a moment ago,' he drawled. 'Besides, isn't that somewhat contradictory in view of the interest you show in those self-same people of the past?' He spread a hand wide to indicate the mines as if in corroboration of his point.

'Not in the slightest,' she took pleasure in refuting. 'There *was* gold to be found in those days—as evidenced by those very mines. It wasn't all wishful thinking, like now.'

'Yet, not long since, you admitted a lot of closures were brought about by reasons other than running out of payable ore.'

'I also said, in most instances it had decreased to a marked extent, though, didn't I?'

'Mmm, but by whose standards? Theirs . . . or

ours?' he countered significantly. 'And who's to say they did locate all the reefs, anyway? Their methods of mining weren't always as thorough, or as scientific, as they might have been.'

'Yes, well, I can see just how much all your thoroughness and modern science has done for you in your eternal—or should that be, infernal?—quest for gold over the years,' she quipped. 'You've made so much out of it that you've managed to rise to the great heights of store assistant!'

Rogan's lips twitched crookedly. 'I've also met a lot of varied and interesting, not to say, nice people. For example, your brother.'

The latter category Kendra didn't doubt she wasn't included in. 'As I'm sure you would also have done if you'd just been content with a more normal occupation,' she contended shortly, and turning, began retracing their steps down the tailings heap.

On solid ground once more she intended to immediately head for home, only to have Rogan enquire leisurely, 'So where to now?'

'There isn't much else to see apart from a couple of derelict old buildings and so forth.' She shrugged uncooperatively. He surely wasn't expecting her to continue as if nothing had happened! 'In any event, I thought you were only interested in the mines and what have you, and I've already shown you where they were all situated.'

'Although I still haven't seen one at close quarters yet, or their associated chimneys,' he pointed out, referring to those tall brickwork stacks that still remained and which had served as flues for the boilers that operated the winding machinery. He inclined his head towards her a little, his expression altering to a chafing one. 'And you did agree to a tour of the *town*.'

So she had—foolishly! But if his kissing her had

patently been of such little consequence to him, then the last thing she wanted to do was to give him any reason to suspect its effect on her had been any greater—which meant of course that she was just going to have to comply. Her decision made, or forced upon her, Kendra sighed fatalistically and set off up the sloping street in the direction of two boarded-up buildings that had housed a bakery and a hardware store in more populous and prosperous times.

After that came a short trip across to the cemetery—always invaluable areas for providing an insight into a town's history, not to mention a record of its diasters, too, on occasion. The Celtic crosses adorning some of the graves being reminders of the Cornishmen who had been among those to flock to the area in the early days, and who had also been the builders of the mine stacks that today stood as plumb as they had when first erected.

Many tombstones related to deaths in the mines. Even more to children who had succumbed to the diseases so typical, and prevalent, in those days before the advent of immunisation; while perhaps only slightly less told of the early demise of young women as a result of childbirth in those hard, pioneering times.

They left the cemetery by way of the more recent sections, and as she passed one particular double grave Kendra automatically stopped for a minute or two in order to pluck the dead blooms from the flowers growing there and to dispose of the few encroaching weeds.

'Your parents?' hazarded Rogan on noting the names chiselled into the stonework.

Her brief labour concluded, she straightened and stood looking down in silent contemplation momentarily before giving an affirmative nod.

'They were both comparatively young,' he remarked quietly. The dates said it all.

'Yes.' She nodded again, an unconsciously wistful note in her voice as she resumed making for the gate.

Rogan walked alongside her meditatively. 'You said your father was killed in the mine,' he recalled. A brief hesitation and he cued softly, 'And your mother . . .?'

Kendra didn't look at him but kept her eyes fixed to the ground in front of her. 'The car she was driving was swept off the causeway that crosses the creek a few miles north of town and she was drowned,' she disclosed as calmly as possible. 'We assume she must have been trying to avoid being stranded on the other side due to more rain having been forecast and . . .' she swallowed painfully, 'it being my fifteenth birthday the following day. If it hadn't been for that I'm sure she would never have attempted it. She was well aware of its treacherous reputation, and the fact that it had already claimed a number of lives over the years.'

Rogan watched her changing expressions intently. 'And what makes you blame yourself for her death?'

'I did for a long time,' she owned with a sigh. 'But I don't any more. At least, I don't think I do.' The addition was accompanied by a weak half smile.

'That also being why you obviously felt it was your duty to take over her role so completely, even to the extent of being responsible for Darby, instead of the other way round, as it should be?'

The unexpected attack, for no matter how dispassionately it may have been uttered that was the only way Kendra could see it, had her head snapping upwards abruptly and a smouldering resentment darkening her blue eyes.

'And if I hadn't taken over from her, who else would have taken care of the house and the store? That damned mine's the only thing my father or

Darby ever wanted to put any effort into! I might point out, however, that neither of them ever seemed to find anything to complain about in my actions!' She halted, her breasts rising and falling rapidly. 'While as for my behaving as if I'm responsible for Darby . . . well, why wouldn't I? If I didn't insist he come home at nights, and spend the weekends at home, he wouldn't leave the mine for weeks, even months, at a time. Nor would he bother making himself any proper meals. In fact, he'd probably forget to eat at all most days . . . as you would undoubtedly know, being of the same unreliable kind yourself!' she concluded with an acidly gibing smile.

Rogan's responding widening of his shapely mouth had her catching her breath in her throat. 'Except that, in my case, although I've certainly done a fair amount of gold mining, both alluvial and reef, as well as enjoyed doing so, *unlike* Darby I've never allowed it to rule my life to the exclusion of all else. A distinction even *you*,' he tapped her beneath the chin in chiding emphasis, 'are finally going to have to make between us one of these days, sweetheart, no matter how opposed you evidently are to the idea for some unaccountable reason.'

Although her head had lifted instinctively at his provoking touch, Kendra at least found it less perturbing, not to mention dismaying, than his previous method of showing there was a decided difference between himself and her brother, and as a result it enabled her to return his gaze nonchalantly.

'Well, then, if there's so much about me that apparently aggravates you so unbearably, there's nothing to prevent you from moving out, you know,' she suggested in honeyed accents. 'I'm positive Genevieve would be only too pleased to provide you with accommodation—and whatever other creature comforts you may desire—at her father's hotel.'

Rogan's eyes narrowed mock threateningly in retaliation for that last comment, but it was the slow grin pulling at the corners of his finely etched mouth that gave Kendra cause for alarm because it was so undeniably irresistible and mesmerising in its effect.

'Uh-uh!' He shook his head lazily. 'Never unbearably. I reckon I can stand it. *And* I'm more than content where I am for the moment.'

Still with her unruly emotions floundering somewhat, in return Kendra could only offer a hopefully indifferent, 'Oh, well, it's your decision, of course.' Then promptly set off at a rapid pace, trusting to have recovered her equilibrium by the time they reached their next point of interest.

CHAPTER FOUR

AT last they were on their way home! sighed Kendra in relief some considerable time later as she and Rogan made their way back to the main street. She was certain he had ensured not a solitary construction, or even the sites of those long-since gone, had been missed in their peregrinations, although his inspections of the mines, poppetheads, and chimney stacks they visited had been the worst as far as she was concerned. Had he really had to study each of them, and the associated pieces of rusty machinery that still existed beside some, in such minute and time-consuming detail?

Her feeling of thankfulness was to be short-lived, though, for as they finally neared the house annoyance, coupled with a deep dismay, immediately replaced it on her observation of a couple of large, and very unwanted presences calmly and methodically devouring her garden.

'Oh, damn! I knew this would happen!' she wailed on a despairing note and, breaking into a run, raced to the gate and around the house into the back yard, dragging off her cap as she went.

By cutting across the vacant ground next door and lithely hurdling the side fence, Rogan made it before she did even so, a couple of well-aimed swipes with his hat across the heads of the two dark red-and-white coated steers successfully persuading them to halt their destructive foraging, if not to immediately take their departure as they sprang a few startled steps away and then just stood eyeing their attacker nervously.

When another, in Kendra's irate form, also arrived on the scene, however, they were soon convinced of the error of their ways and were soon herded through the gaping breach in the back fence they had pushed down to gain entrance. Although not before having trampled indiscriminately over most of the vegetable patches, bringing forth further recriminations and lamentations from Kendra in the process.

With their exit, Rogan set about doing what he could to restore the fence to, if not an upright position—it was some years since it had been in that good a state—then at least closer to a sloping resemblance of it than had been the case after the cattle had finished with it.

'If you let me know where Darby keeps his tools, I'll repair that properly for you this afternoon,' he surprised Kendra by stating casually once he had done all he could with it. 'As it is, they'll be back in here again the minute they get the chance.'

'I know.' She grimaced dolefully. 'Only you don't have to mend it. That—that's not part of your job.' A self-consciousness began edging into her voice. She wasn't sure she wanted to be beholden to him for anything. 'But thank you for your efforts in getting rid of *them*.' With an eloquent glance towards the steers who were still standing close by, gazing at the garden with what seemed to be sorrowful eyes at having been deprived of such new and tasty feed.

'Hardly much of an effort,' discounted Rogan with a shrug. A rueful look was directed towards the ravages inflicted on her vegetables. 'I rather think it's going to require more work rectifying that than it did chasing those two out. While as for fixing the fence, just think of it as a return favour for your services as a guide this morning, if you prefer.'

Unfortunately that didn't make her feel any better,

especially when she recalled her initial reluctance and then her attempts to make the tour as brief as possible. 'I wasn't expecting anything in . . .' she began diffidently.

'Oh, for heaven's sake!' he broke in on her in wry exasperation, shaking his head. 'Do you want the fence mended, or don't you?'

'Well—yes—of course I do,' she owned awkwardly. She could hardly have claimed otherwise. 'But . . .'

'Then for crying out loud, stop trying to find objections, will you?' he interrupted drily once more. 'I wouldn't have offered if I hadn't meant it. Besides, you're just wasting time that could be more beneficially utilised, because I don't know about you,' a beguiling smile suddenly made an appearance, 'but I'm dying for something to eat.'

Taken completely unawares, first by that so-disarming smile and then by his words, Kendra only felt capable of countering by sniping, albeit without any real sting, 'Men! Do you ever think of anything apart from what goes into your stomachs—solid . . . or liquid?'

'Mmm, quite often,' Rogan drawled, his eyes compelling as they locked with hers. 'In fact, you could be surprised.'

For a moment Kendra couldn't tear her gaze away as she stared at him in confusion, her heart starting to thump so loudly she thought he must hear it. Then, with a convulsive gulp, she just managed to push out a strangled half laugh.

'I doubt it,' she disputed with something of a croak, and whirling, made for the house as quickly as she could on legs that abruptly seemed to have become decidedly unsteady.

After a salad lunch Rogan returned to the garden immediately, needing to start on the fence straight away if he was to have any chance of completing it by nightfall, for their meal had indeed been a late one. Kendra followed him a short time later, after having pottered aimlessly about the house for a while in an attempt to avoid being anywhere in his vicinity for the remainder of the day, but eventually conceding she really had very little option. If they wanted fresh vegetables she was just going to have to remedy the havoc wreaked on her garden, and the sooner the better. The fact that Rogan was undeniably beginning to turn her life and her emotions upside down she was simply going to have to surmount, or ignore—somehow.

Not that she actually succeeded in doing either that afternoon, she ruefully had to admit after a time spent diligently pulling out those plants the steers had ruined totally and resurrecting those they had merely trodden on, because no matter how hard she tried to concentrate on what she was doing, every time she lifted her head her eyes would unconsciously drift in Rogan's direction. To the extent that, in the end, she resigned herself to the inevitable and, sitting back on her heels as she knelt, allowed her gaze to remain on him, if covertly, and her thoughts to flow unimpeded.

Without a covering shirt—that had already been discarded before she put in an appearance—the mahogany-coloured skin of his muscular back and arms glistened with a fine film of sweat beneath the still-blazing sun as he rammed into position the steel stakes that were to replace the rotted, old wooden ones, and Kendra watched the interplay of those muscles musingly. She was fascinated by his air of rock-hard durability, the tremendous aura of over-whelming strength and power he exuded as he worked, the movements that were as sweeping and self-assured as the man himself.

Yes, there were differences, vital differences, between he and Darby, she suddenly found herself allowing. For although her brother wasn't averse to lending a hand when it was needed—as shown by his assistance to Vivian—she still knew without a doubt that he would never apply himself with such single-minded dedication to something that held no engrossing interest for him, such as his mine, whereas she strongly suspected Rogan would give his all no matter what he undertook.

'Well, do I pass muster?' The lightly amused query interrupted Kendra's reverie, causing her to start and bringing a quick rush of colour to her face on realising she had been discovered staring at him so fixedly. Leaning one arm on the post he had just sunk, Rogan removed his hat with his other hand, wiped his arm across his forehead and settled the wide-brimmed covering back into place before continuing in the same wry tone, 'Or have you some complaint to make about the way it's progressing?'

'N-no, of course I haven't,' she denied in a flustered stammer. Well, not about how the fence was progressing, she didn't, at least. And in the hope of excusing her absorbed interest in him, 'I was just waiting for—for an opportune moment to ask if you'd like a drink of some kind.' Already scrambling to her feet.

'Any time's opportune in this heat,' he drawled in iron accents. 'And something cold would be extremely welcome right now, I must admit.'

'Anything in particular?' she asked over her shoulder as she thankfully took the opportunity to leave before any other excuses may have been required, then uttered a slightly self-mocking laugh and pulled a sardonic face. 'No, don't bother to tell me—I already know.'

'Now that's what I like to see ... an instant understanding of a fellow being's needs.'

The bantering call behind her had Kendra neither replying nor looking back. She was too busy railing at herself for having permitted her thoughts to return to his first question and, worse, answer it with an affirmative. Yes, he did indeed pass muster. It wasn't a concession she had wanted, or even expected, to ever make.

When she returned, Rogan was sitting with his back against the trunk of a shading tree just outside the fence, his long legs drawn up and his forearms resting across his knees, a lighted cigarette held in his hand.

'Thanks.' He smiled his appreciation on her handing him his can of beer in a foam plastic container, and pulling back the tab took a long, and obviously much welcome swallow. He then indicated his cigarette with a dip of his head, his brows rising questioningly. 'Do you smoke?'

'Occasionally.' She shrugged.

'Then make this one of those times, and sit and talk to me,' he partly instructed, partly urged, and much to her surprise. Nodding towards his shirt that was draped over another post a little further along, he offered, 'Help yourself. They're in the pocket.'

Shifting restlessly from one foot to the other, Kendra hesitated, uncertain of the wisdom of doing as he suggested, then suddenly found her decision seemingly made for her as her legs began carrying her towards the post as if of their own volition.

'What did you want to talk about?' she enquired a little dubiously on having lit herself a cigarette and sinking to the ground beside a dusty-leaved bush a few feet away from him.

He flexed a broad shoulder idly. 'Anything that comes to mind, I guess.' His eyes strayed to the two steers that still hadn't left the area, apparently in the hope of being able to push their way into the garden once more when the hindering humans had departed. 'So whose cattle are they? Yours?'

'Oh, no, they're Alec Smith's,' she supplied, feeling easier as a result of the uncontentious topic. 'He's got a property of some twenty thousand acres, of which we form part of the southern boundary. He's also who we buy our beef on the hoof from and then have it killed and cut up by Frank Edgar, the butcher here in town.' She took a mouthful from her own can of soft drink and smiled impishly as she looked out across the sun-baked bush. 'And there won't be any contest as to which one will be next to fill our freezer, I can tell you.'

'One of those?' Rogan deduced with a laugh, gesturing with his can towards their two earlier intruders.

'Mmm, the baldy faced one, yellow ear tag number 147. He's always hanging around here munching on any of my shrubs that happen to grow over the fence, or that he can reach through the wire. Not for much longer, though. Soon we'll be eating *him* instead.'

'Bloodthirsty little devil, aren't you?' he grinned.

'Well, someone's going to eat him anyway, so I figured it may as well be us. A sort of return compliment, if you like.' Her lips curved incorrigibly again.

For a moment or two Rogan's eyes remained fixed on that wide and animated shaping of her mobile mouth, whereupon her smile promptly began to falter and she licked at her lips in sudden self-consciousness.

'So when are you going to tie the knot with Mike Warden?' he asked abruptly at length, dropping his gaze to the lighted tip of his cigarette.

Taken aback a little by the rapid change in subject

as much as the question itself, Kendra answered instinctively. 'So who said I was going to tie the knot with him at all?'

'Well, aren't you?' He shot her a deeply speculative look.

Unused to discussing her private life in anything but the broadest terms, she elevated her slim nose to a defiant angle. 'Not that it's any concern of yours . . . but no, not to my knowledge,' she refuted stiffly, although without quite understanding why she should still have been so forthcoming anyway.

'From his attitude last night, I gained the impression . . .'

'Then you're obviously labouring under the same misapprehension he is!' she cut in with a snap and took a quick draw on her cigarette. He was meaning Mike's proprietorial and jealously antagonistic attitude, she supposed, giving a disgruntled grimace.

'Yet I would have thought he more than adequately filled all your criteria.' Rogan proceeded to muse in a tone faintly laced with mockery, and evidently, or perhaps deliberately, refusing to take the hint that she had no wish to discuss her relationship with the other man further. 'After all, he's clearly a solid pillar of the community, responsible, dependable, a respectable businessman with no likely financial problems either now or in the future, and certainly not subject to that most execrable weakness . . . an interest in gold prospecting.' He paused briefly and his dusky-edged, smoky-green eyes filled with lazy taunting. 'From your point of view, a perfect paragon, no less, I would've said. So where does he fail your requirements . . . in bed?'

'H-how dare you!' Kendra spluttered wrathfully, her face warming with an ungovernable heat. It wasn't even as if she had been interested enough in Mike to want to go to bed with him anyway, or any other man for that matter. Not that she had any intention of revealing as much, however. 'None of this is any of your damned business! Although I am glad to note that you do realise that Mike at least has a number of virtues . . . which is more than can be said for some!' Shades of caustic sarcasm began stealing into her voice.

Rogan smiled obliquely, imperturbed, took a casual drink from his can, and shrugged. 'Then why *aren't* you marrying him?'

'Because I don't happen to want to! Because I don't love him, that's why!' vexation pushed her into divulging involuntarily. An admission she immediately sought to put behind her by rushing on to gibe, 'You know, that emotion you, and others like you, reserve solely for that glittering yellow metal in the ground!'

'Uh-uh!' He shook his head in drawling, laughing denial. 'As I told you earlier, sweetheart, I've never allowed it to rule my life completely—and especially not to the stage of excluding the fairer sex. I've always managed to find time for them.'

As any number of them had for him too, she didn't doubt. 'Although not to the point of marrying one of them obviously!'

'You'd have me inflict my so unworthy self on one of your kind?' he countered, facetiously reproving.

'Mmm, I guess that would be asking just too much for someone to bear, wouldn't it?' She didn't hesitate to agree in acid tones, even if it was in total contradiction of her wayward thoughts—to the effect that undoubtedly some members of her own sex wouldn't have cared less what he did for a living if only he would take more than a passing interest in them. The idea made her feel strangely dissatisfied and she stubbed out her cigarette roughly on a patch of dry earth. 'And now . . .' She began climbing to her feet. 'I think I'd better get back to what I was doing or I won't get it all done today. If you've finished with your can I'll put it in the garbage for you.' She felt obliged to offer since that was where she would be first heading in order to dispose of her own.

Draining the last of his beer, Rogan gained his own feet smoothly, and handed the empty container over to her with an acknowledging, 'Thanks.' Then, as she half turned to leave, he caught her lightly by the nape of the neck, halting her progress. 'And for the thought in providing it,' he added quietly, tilting her head inexorably up to his and brushing his mouth against hers briefly.

He released her again almost immediately and without a word Kendra hurriedly made her departure. It had only been a fleeting contact, but the memory of it, and the knowledge that she had nevertheless spontaneously responded, remained with her for too long afterwards for her to be able to disregard its effect on her as readily, or as reassuringly, as she would have wished.

In fact, she was quite at a loss as to how to even satisfactorily explain the general effect just his presence seemed to have on her most of the time, let alone any closer, more disquieting contact. He was disturbing her life in a way no one ever had before, and she found it not only somewhat perplexing but decidedly perturbing as well. Particularly when the sensations Rogan aroused within her with such apparent ease were all so unfamiliar and difficult to analyse.

In the days that followed, however, as she both lived and worked alongside him, it eventually became impossible for Kendra not to recognise and admit, no matter how reluctantly, just why Rogan's dark, compelling attraction affected her to such a degree and why she was equally unable to discount it. She had illogically fallen in love with him—a prospector!—and the more so as each day passed it appeared. Her whole life suddenly seemed to revolve around him, her every waking thought, and some of her sleeping ones, too, filled with images of him, the mere sight of him sufficient to set her pulse racing chaotically.

Now she could understand why Maureen had so readily forgotten her vow never to become involved with a gold miner, because despite all her self-censure for having allowed such a senseless thing to happen, even if unconsciously, she knew very well in her heart that she would more than likely have done exactly as her friend had and married the man if given half the chance. The only trouble being, in Kendra's case, that she clearly wasn't to be afforded that chance, because someone else entirely was already eagerly staking a claim, and with Rogan's approval apparently. Genevieve!

The petite redhead was an almost daily visitor to the store now, sometimes for hours at a time, her continual invitations for Rogan to join her for dinner and/or lunch at the hotel, to drive with her to Red Gap on the weekend, or simply to meet her at one of the waterholes in Saddlebag Creek for a swim after work, ensuring his attention had no opportunity to stray.

Not that he ever appeared to object, Kendra had no choice but to own, despondently. At the same time it made it all the more imperative that she keep her own feelings from showing—it was the least she could do if she wanted to retain any of her pride and self-respect at all—regardless of the mounting despair and gnawing jealousy (there was no other way to describe it) generated by seeing them together so often and in such cheerful accord.

As a result, though, her own manner became even more critical and gibing than usual, her whole attitude defensive for fear of what she might accidentally allow someone to suspect, her temper shortening so much due to her frayed emotions that even Darby was prompted into chipping her about it.

'For God's sake, Kendra, what's got into you?' he remonstrated one morning after Rogan had just left the breakfast table, and raking his hand through his hair distractedly. 'You're as touchy as a publican at closing time these days! I thought having Rogan to help you out in the store would enable you to take things easier. Instead, you seem determined to force him into leaving. I mean to say, just what was that last crack for, hmm? Or isn't anyone supposed to ask?' He shook his head ruefully. 'I tell you, love, you continue to carry on as you have been doing of late and one of these times . . .' He shook his head again, but this time in warning. 'You could very well find you've bitten off more than you can chew where Rogan's concerned. He isn't going to take it as well as he has to date for ever, you know.' He stretched out a hand to touch her arm, his expression becoming entreating. 'So how about giving him a fair go, even if it is only for my sake, huh? I reckon you'd find a lot to like about him if only you'd forget his prospecting background for a while.'

Kendra half shrugged vaguely, wistfully. If he did but know, she already liked Rogan too much for her own good as it was! Which was precisely why she was having to keep up her charade, in spite of everything inside her rebelling at the idea. Because in view of how matters stood she simply couldn't bear the thought of anyone—Rogan, in particular—discovering just how radically her feelings towards him *had* altered!

'You promise?' Darby now queried on a happier note, apparently having taken her hunched shoulder as an indication of agreement.

Rather than answer directly—she couldn't give an affirmative reply, and doubted her ability to convincingly explain a negative one—she merely gave an indeterminate half smile in lieu and hoped he would draw his own conclusions as before. And from the openly satisfied and relieved grin she received in return it seemed he had.

None the less, as more time passed and it became increasingly clear that Rogan's tolerance did indeed have limits—truth to tell, she had been as surprised as Darby that he'd accepted her taunting remarks as well and for as long as he had—Kendra was finally compelled to conclude that if she wasn't more prudent with the keen edge of her tongue, then she very shortly could be feeling even more wretched than she did already.

For a while she succeeded, too, although only by taking the completely opposite tack and hardly talking at all except when it was absolutely necessary. Or at least she succeeded until the night some two weeks or so later when, after having spent the evening with Maureen and Jon at their small house, she arrived home to discover another mud-and-dust-covered Land Cruiser sporting Northern Territory number-plates parked behind Rogan's identical vehicle at the side of the house and a casually, but well-dressed, grey haired man of some fifty-odd years seated in one of the old cane chairs on the verandah.

Wondering who he could be and what he could be wanting at that late hour, Kendra mounted the steps towards him with a slight frown pulling her finely marked brows together. 'Good evening. Is there something . . .' she began enquiringly, but only to break off as, on rising to his feet at her appearance, the stranger also began to speak at the same time.

'Ah, an arrival!' he exclaimed in amiable, satisfied tones. 'I was beginning to think no one would ever come. And if you're wondering who in blazes I am, which I'm sure you must be,' accompanied by a wry chuckle, 'the name's Faulkner, Curran Faulkner, and the reason I'm here is because I'm looking for my son. I was told at the pub that he was staying here.'

'You're Rogan's father?' Kendra gasped, unable to keep her astonishment out of her voice. Apart from his weather-darkened skin he certainly didn't look like any old-time, itinerant gold prospector she'd ever seen! For one thing, his clothes were far too expensive looking.

'That's me all right,' he confirmed drily. 'And you're . . .?' His iron grey brows lifted to a quizzical peak.

'Oh, I'm sorry, I should have said,' she apologised a trifle self-consciously. 'Actually, I'm Kendra Onslow. My brother, Darby, and I own the house and the store next door.' She paused. 'I'm also sorry there was no one home when you first arrived, but Rogan and Darby should be back shortly. Well, they *said* they didn't expect to be too late, but when Darby and his mates get together . . .' She gave a meaningful grimace.

'I understand.' Curran Faulkner's lips twitched humorously. 'But at least I do now know where my son is. Of course, as to why he's here is another matter.' Suddenly, he slanted her a subtle gaze. 'Or would I be right in thinking you could be the reason?'

'Me!' Kendra half gulped, half squeaked, her cheeks burning hotly. She only wished it were true. 'Oh, no—no, his being here has nothing to do with me. He—he's just staying with us because he took up Darby's offer of a job working in the store, that's all.'

'A job? Working in a store?' It was plain the revelation had taken her listener noticeably aback. 'For heaven's sake, what on earth for?' He shook his head in disbelief.

His incredulity had her own earlier frown returning in full force. 'Because he—he needed one, we supposed,' she faltered uncertainly. 'Didn't he write and let you know?'

Curran Faulkner's expression assumed a distinctly ironic cast. 'I haven't had a word from Rogan since he left our operation in the Gulf to come down here in order to check on the work being conducted on the old Southern Cross Consolidated mining lease. And that's almost six weeks ago now! Normally, that wouldn't concern me greatly, I must admit—it wouldn't be the first time Rogan's taken off into the bush without warning if he thinks there's something worth investigating—but when I contacted the camp and was informed he'd left there some time ago with the intention of returning north, or so he had advised at the time, only for them to have since received further notification that he was still in Goldfield but that they shouldn't acknowledge him if one of them chanced to see him, then I figured it was time I found out for myself just exactly what in hell *is* going on.'

At his mention of the local mine Kendra's nerves had tightened like coiling springs, her emotions starting to seethe ungovernably. So he had merely decided to look the place over because he'd just happened to be in north Queensland, had he? The conniving, two-faced liar!

'In that regard, I don't suppose you'd be able to help, would you?' Rogan's parent went on hopefully, interrupting her fuming reverie.

'No, I don't really think so,' she denied shortly, even though she had her own very definite suspicions on the subject. 'Apart from mentioning that the two of you, yourself in particular, had done a fair amount of prospecting in your time, he didn't see fit to divulge much else about anything!' Then, stricken with a sense of remorse for her acrimonious reply—it wasn't Curran Faulkner's fault his son was such an unscrupulous, deceiving louse, when all was said and done—she attempted to make amends by offering politely, 'But please, come into the house while you wait for him, won't you, Mr Faulkner?' Pulling open the flyscreen door that was never locked, and pausing only to switch on a light, she proceeded to lead the way to the kitchen. 'I'm sure you could do with a cup of tea or coffee after your wait. Perhaps something to eat even.'

'No, just a cup of tea will do me, thank you. As a matter of fact, I had quite a pleasant meal at the hotel before I came down here ... as well as a most vivacious young female to keep me company while I ate it,' he added with a laugh, taking the chair proferred. 'From what she had to say, I gather she knows Rogan quite well too.'

'Probably better than anyone else in town,' Kendra put forward sardonically with a scowl for the kettle she was putting on the stove. Trust Genevieve, for it was undoubtedly her Curran Faulkner was referring to, to have ferreted out and promptly put to good use for her own purpose, the identity of this particular newcomer to Goldfield.

'Oh?'

The partly surprised, partly questioning exclamation from behind her in response to her comment had her shrugging deprecatingly, but not turning around as she occupied herself taking cups and saucers from the cupboard. She was a little perplexed, though, as to how Rogan's father could possibly have thought she herself may have been the reason for his son remaining in town when Genevieve must have made it abundantly obvious she was the one who had all his attention.

'Yes, well, I guess Rogan's the best one to ask about that,' she temporised finally. Following it with a deviating, 'Do you take sugar and milk, Mr Faulkner?'

'Mmm, whenever possible.' His assent was punctuated by a laugh. 'Too often we've had to do without both when camped in the bush.' He continued genially, 'I'd be pleased if you'd just make it Curry, though. I haven't been mistered since I can't remember when, and to be honest, I much prefer informality.'

Kendra nodded understandingly. It was always the same in the bush. 'But ... Curry?' She eyed him curiously. 'Didn't you say, Curran, when you introduced yourself?'

'Yes, well, that is my proper name,' he granted. 'However, I was also born at the 'Curry—Cloncurry—near the Territory border, and I guess the similarity between the two names was just too much to ignore, so Curry I've always been ever since I can remember.'

'I see.' She smiled as she filled the teapot, and placing it on the table, took the seat opposite him. Hesitating, she then pushed on regardless, if a touch diffidently. 'Although I understand you've actually lived in the Territory for some years now.'

'That's right. Since I was eight or nine, in fact.'

Kendra poured their tea contemplatively, her thoughts returning to that which had set her smouldering previously. 'And it's just you who's—er—investigating the possibilities of the Southern Cross mine, is it?'

'Well, Rogan's and my corporation, anyway.' The qualification came matter-of-factly.

Not even a mere company! Kendra noted tartly. 'And your operation in the Gulf? I gather, then, that it's quite—umm—successful?' she probed in tight accents.

There was a sudden flash of white teeth. 'Oh, my word, yes,' Curry relayed unequivocally. 'We've been open cut mining for some years now and it's been yielding some eighteen to twenty thousand ounces of gold annually. Not as much as some of the larger consortiums are getting in places, of course, but certainly extremely pleasing results for a privately owned concern.'

And why wouldn't it be pleasing! At current prices, that amount would immediately have elevated both him and his son very much into the millionaire class after only one year! she realised with a swallow on doing some rough calculations. No wonder Curran Faulkner didn't look like the usual run of struggling prospectors! And no wonder his son had shown so little interest in the happenings at the Southern Cross mine, too! the rancorous thought followed. An indifference that had puzzled her somewhat at the time. The dissembling snake in the grass had known precisely what was taking place out there all along of course!

'So now you're hoping to do the same here, is that it?' she half asked, half charged, unable to rid herself entirely of her feelings of animosity and bitterness at Rogan's duplicity.

'Better, actually, in view of the results of the tests we've undertaken,' he confounded her a little by disclosing. She was still reluctant to believe the area hadn't been worked out long ago. 'Although I trust you'll keep that information to yourself, naturally,' he continued at once. 'As we're only just preparing to submit our applications for the necessary leases I would prefer it if it didn't become common knowledge until everything's been finalised officially.'

'Oh, I don't think you need to worry about anyone here in Goldfield doing anything that would jeopardise your undertaking. That's not our style,' she defended. 'It would appear underhand dealings seem to come more naturally to outsiders!' The edge of sarcasm in her voice increased markedly.

A nuance that didn't go unnoticed either apparently, for Curry's lips promptly took on a rueful tilt. 'I'm beginning to think I may have done Rogan a great disservice by arriving as unexpectedly as I have, because unless I miss my guess, by doing so I've—er—put him right in it, haven't I?'

Right up to his deserving-of-being-stretched neck! gritted Kendra inwardly. Aloud, she simply disclaimed defensively with as offhand a hunching of a slender shoulder as she could manage, 'I don't know why you'd think that. After all, we're nothing to him, so why should he justify himself to us?'

'But you still feel you've been duped, and that hurts, hmm?'

The shrewd assessment had her dropping her gaze to the cup before her, unexpected tears abruptly stinging her eyes, but which she blinked back rapidly. Yes, it hurt—unbearably—and for more reasons than he would ever know. When she finally raised her head again, however, her features were carefully schooled once more, but before she could speak the sound of feet crossing the verandah to the back door had her inhaling a jagged breath instead, and she was undecided as to whether she was relieved or distressed by the imminent interruption.

Notwithstanding, one wryly guarded look in her

direction from Rogan after he'd finished greeting his parent and introducing him to Darby was sufficient to have the light of battle returning to her blue eyes.

'I thought it must have been you when we saw the Cruiser parked round the side,' Rogan went on, turning a chair round in order to straddle it casually, his crossed arms resting lightly on the back, and thereby explaining his lack of surprise on coming face to face with his father. 'What time did you arrive?'

'Oh, a few hours ago,' Curry advised airily, and then fixed his son with a sardonic gaze. 'Since you'd been gone for so long—without a word, I might add— I thought it just could be advisable to come down and ensure that you *were* still in the land of the living.'

'Very much so, as you can see,' grinned Rogan impenitently. Pausing, his darkly fringed eyes flicked in Kendra's direction once again as she retrieved more china from the cupboard. 'And Kendra's been keeping you entertained while you've been waiting, has she?'

'More the opposite, actually.' It was Kendra herself who answered in a deceptively sweet voice as she thumped rather than placed a cup and saucer beside him. 'You just wouldn't believe how positively riveting I found the information your father had to impart. As I'm sure Darby will, too.' The addition was made with a little less sweetness, but a whole lot more emphasis.

Rogan's mouth sloped crookedly as, this time, his gaze was slanted expressively at his father, who responded with an equally explicit one, though apologetically so in his case.

Darby, meanwhile, looked to his sister enquiringly. 'Oh, and what's that? It certainly sounds interesting.'

'Oh, it is, I can assure you,' she had no compunction in verifying as she passed him his cup and saucer in turn. 'Quite a revelation, in fact, you might say. Especially the part about *why* our new employee just happens to be in this area!' Her eyes locked contemptuously with a pair of intent grey-green ones across the table.

'I don't follow you.' Darby gave a frowning shake of his head, both sounding and looking totally baffled.

'Then I suggest you get Rogan to explain it all to you,' she proposed caustically. 'He seems to be the only one with all the answers! Of course, whether he'll actually tell you the truth, even this time, is something else again, though!'

From across the table came an explosive epithet as Rogan swung to his feet so swiftly that for the moment Kendra was stunned into immobility. 'Right, spitfire! You want a collection of dues, you can bloody well have one! Your efforts to crowd me have finally paid off!' he grated, and grabbing hold of her wrist in a none too gentle grip he proceeded to haul her as yet still shocked form around the table and towards the doorway leading into the hall.

'Rogan!' His father immediately frowned, half rising from his chair.

'Oh, don't worry, she'll still be in one piece when I've finished,' came the satirically worded reply. And sparing a meaningful glance for Darby, 'It's been coming, mate.'

Her brother's ruefully endorsing expression was more than sufficient to have Kendra fully recovering her wits and with a partly indignant, partly baleful glare for his disloyalty, she launched into fuming speech even as she was dragged from the room.

'Let go of my arm, Rogan Faulkner!' she blazed, hitting out with her free hand and catching him on the shoulder. 'Just who do you think you are to treat me in such an arrogant fashion! I'll have you know . . .'

'And I'll have you know that I've taken as much as I

damn well intend to from you! You cantankerous, intolerant, little shrew!' he interposed savagely and spun her away from him dismissively on their reaching the sitting room at the front of the house where he switched on the light in a furious motion.

Kendra drew in a sharp breath at the uncomplimentary description, ignoring her smarting wrist. 'Meaning, you can't *take* the truth either . . . as well as not being able to tell it?' she dared to gibe witheringly in retaliation.

For a long moment their eyes clashed and battled across the scant space that separated them, and then Rogan muttered something violent under his breath. 'Except that you're such a waspish bigot with your own personal axe to grind that it's extremely doubtful you would even *know* the truth, let alone admit it, if it was staring you in the face!' he ground out no less scorchingly.

'And where you're concerned, with perfect justification I would have thought, since you've been worming your way into everyone's confidence under false pretences right from the time you accepted Darby's offer of work!' She uttered a short, derogatory, half laugh. 'Making out you were just another down-and-out prospector, when all the time you were actually anything but!'

'Then considering your views regarding the former, I would have expected your reaction to be something quite different on finding I'm not!' Pausing, his mouth took on a cynical, derisive upturn. 'Or is that what's really cheesing you off? Because it incontrovertibly, not to say infuriatingly, puts paid to your prejudiced theory about there being no more gold to be won from the old fields?'

Until then Kendra hadn't actually realised their Gulf operation was on a previously worked goldfield, but that was the least of her concerns at present. 'Whether it does or not has nothing to do with it, so you needn't think you're going to twist everything around in an effort to divert attention from your own despicable behaviour by making it appear as if I've something to answer for!' she jeered. 'You're the one who's been playing us all for suckers, not me!'

'Merely by failing to reveal that I wasn't as down on my luck as you supposed?' he mocked, though still in a taut voice.

'Not to mention the reason for doing so, of course! Just because we may live in a backwater, doesn't necessarily make us back*ward*, you know! Do you think I'm not aware of just what's been behind this whole rotten charade of yours? That it's simply been a vile attempt to secretly pump Darby, and other poor unsuspecting fools like him, for their local knowledge of those areas they consider have a good chance of bearing gold so that, if it sounds worthwhile, you can get the jump on them, because you can afford it, by taking out the appropriate claims and leases before they do, as well as, for all I know, convincing them to give up their own mines which would then allow you to lay claim to the whole damned area without hindrance!'

A muscle jerked beneath Rogan's sun-bronzed cheek, his eyes hardening to pure green chips of ice, all semblance of his customary amiable nature lost beneath a rigidly controlled rage. 'If you were a man I'd knock you into next week for that!' he grated on a harshly rasping note. 'But in any event, I wouldn't be as rashly tempted into making any such preposterous charges again, if I were you, or . . .' a hand abruptly sank within the curls of her hair, forcing her face upwards and inexorably closer to his, 'you may still find yourself getting more than you bargain for! So be warned!' He gave her hair a sharply emphasising tug before freeing her again.

'And so had you better be, too!' Kendra immediately fired back defiantly despite the momentary feeling of apprehension that had assailed her on seeing that grim, cold mask of anger settling over his face, giving him a dangerous and unexpectedly ruthless air. 'Because no matter how preposterous you might claim it to be, I notice you still didn't deny anything I said! And when Darby also hears the true reason for your being here ...!' She left the sentence significantly unfinished.

'I'll be very surprised if he doesn't accept it with a great deal more tolerance and far less irrationality than you!' he proposed in biting tones.

'Irrationality!' Her blue eyes sparked with acrimony. 'You call it irrational to object to being deliberately fed a diet of lies?'

'When it wasn't anything of the kind ... what else?' he countered with a snap. 'Because, for your information, failing to reveal my whole background does not constitute lying! Although, in your case, perhaps perverse or just plain contrary *would* have been more apt descriptions!'

'Is that so?' she heaved with seething resentment.

'Precisely!' His facetious affirmation was drenched in heavy sarcasm. 'Because after all these weeks of listening to your mocking comments about useless, wishful thinking prospectors, it now appears to cause you more irritation to discover a successful one! And not only that, but *if*,' his tone was trenchantly accented, 'it had been my intention to somehow deprive Darby of his mine for which you know bloody well compensation would need to be paid anyway— then considering those very same views of yours about him leading such a wasteful life in even searching for gold at all, just what would *you* call your present attitude of outrage at the idea of him not doing so in future . . . if not perverse and contrary, hmm?' He quirked a derisive brow expressively high.

The insufferably satiric timbre in his voice both grated and rankled, and as a result had her venturing to reciprocate recklessly. 'I'd call it an unwillingness to see him cheated out of what's rightfully his by someone who masquerades as a friend solely for their own nefarious ends!'

In the uneasy, tension-vibrating silence that ensued Rogan drew an irate breath, his eyes glittering with a fairly murderous look that had Kendra compulsively moving backwards as a feeling of pure panic invaded her stomach.

'Then as I apparently already have the game, there seems little reason not to also have the game . . . for equally nefarious purposes in other directions too!' he bit out infuriatedly, if a trifle enigmatically from Kendra's viewpoint, his powerful arms suddenly jerking her without warning into a crushing hold as his mouth came down on hers savagely.

There was no following softening in the contact either, only a thoroughly punishing roughness that hurt both physically and mentally and brought unbidden tears to her eyes. She did so wish that things might have been different. But it obviously wasn't to be, and as Rogan's lips continued to grind against hers so unsparingly she belatedly tried to wrest herself from his grasp. As if to prove his total dominance, however, it was Rogan who perceptibly thrust her away, not vice versa, when he finally allowed a parting to occur.

'And now, unless you care for more of the same, I suggest you keep your accusations to yourself in future, and in turn, yourself out of my way!' he recommended on a taut, hard-edged note.

It brought about a return of Kendra's own anger, although the almost feverishly bright gaze she fixed him with gave an unknowingly luminous glow to eyes that still shimmered with tears as yet unshed. 'While *you* can get out of this house, and forget about the store as well!' she retorted fierily.

For a fraction of a second Rogan didn't reply as his narrowed glance continued to hold hers intently, and then with an unconcerned flexing of a wide shoulder he inclined his dark head in a sardonic salute. 'It will be my pleasure,' he asserted tersely, and began heading for the doorway with a purposeful stride.

Kendra watched him go with her head angled high but with a swelling ache in her heart that threatened to suffocate her, and hastily leaving the room herself now, she made for her bedroom. Once there, she promptly collapsed on to her bed, the tears she had previously managed to hold at bay now starting to course down her cheeks unchecked as she gave way to the anguish and sorrow that swept over her in uncontrollable waves.

As lacerated and raw as she felt at his behaviour and duplicity, she still knew there could never be anyone else for her—no matter how she might wish it otherwise. Her thoughts were made all the more depressing, even if Rogan had unwittingly assumed her to have been irritated, on having learnt that he was a successful prospector. For having made the comment that she would never become involved with one, how could she ever appear to reverse that opinion after having discovered him to be a wealthy one? There was only one conclusion everyone, including Rogan, could ever draw from that!

With the ache in her chest becoming a tightening ball of misery, Kendra turned her tear-streaked face into her pillow, the muted sound of voices emanating from the kitchen penetrating her consciousness briefly and making her catch at her lower lip with even white teeth in distracted contemplation.

In view of her brother's evident regard for Rogan, at least that was prior to his underhandedness coming to light, she couldn't help but wonder just what Darby's reaction would be to hearing she had not only ordered Rogan from the house but fired him as well. Would he endorse her dictates, dispute them, or worse . . . over-rule them? No, it couldn't possibly be the latter, she swiftly tried to allay the apprehension that thought aroused. Not even he could be tolerant of deceit to that extent, surely! That he might dispute her precipitate manner in having done so was a very real possibility, though, she had to concede, forlornly. But that was something only the morning would tell.

CHAPTER FIVE

Since it was a work day and, not surprisingly, she hadn't slept particularly well anyway, Kendra rose early the next morning and on her way to the kitchen chanced a hasty look into the room Rogan usually occupied, whereupon disconcertingly confused feelings, partly of relief and partly of loss, made their presence felt on finding it completely bare of both him and his possessions. With a sigh she continued on her way, trying determinedly to invest herself with a composure she was actually far from experiencing.

She had already made a pot of tea and was in the middle of grilling some bacon when she heard rather than saw Darby's entrance into the room and, resolving to get what obviously needed to be said out of the way as soon as possible—apart from considering attack being the best form to take, just in case some defence on her part was required—Kendra ensured she was the first to speak.

'Well, your Territorian mate certainly turned out to be a beauty, didn't he?' she charged with a sardonic grimace, and a touch of defiance in her stance as she turned to face him.

'As did my sister,' he wasn't averse to drawling wryly.

Kendra stiffened, but swung back to the stove with a show of supposed unconcern. 'Meaning?'

'That right from the beginning you went out of your way not to give him a chance,' he supplied, exhaling a heavily regretful breath.

'To do what?' She spun back again to counter tartly.

'Pick your brains, and then probably your pocket as well by taking over the Good Cheer when your lease comes up for renewal, if he thought it profitable?'

Darby gave his head an incredulous shake. 'Oh, don't be ridiculous, love!' he admonished. 'It's a bit harder than that to take over an already recorded claim these days ... as you should know,' he argued drily. 'Besides, most questions Rogan ever asked me were really about the area as a whole, certainly not in regard to any specific mine or claim.'

'Then if he had nothing to hide, why all the secrecy? Why not reveal exactly who he was and why he was here? And more particularly, why take a job he didn't need, especially as he obviously couldn't have meant keeping it long anyhow ... if there *wasn't* something sly going on?'

'As to why he took the job—well—I gather that did have something to do with providing a handy, not to say novel, opportunity to get some additional information, plus background, on the area without anyone being aware precisely why he was in the district,' he advised. But on seeing Kendra about to jump in triumphantly, hurried on to explain, 'Although not for any sinister reason as you immediately suspected.'

'Oh?' Not only her voice but her expression as well was patently sceptical.

'Uh-huh,' Darby maintained with a trace of a laugh. 'And I can't say I blame him either, because I reckon I might have done the same if I'd been in his place. Because *he*,' stressed pointedly as he eyed her with subtle irony 'and which I'm surprised didn't occur to you when you learnt in just what connection he really was here, was more interested in the locals' likely reaction to the operation going ahead, and especially so close to town, because it only seems to require a concerted demonstration or two these days and you know what the result can be. A hold up for God knows how long until it's sorted out to everyone's satisfaction—if ever.'

'So he decided to do some undercover public relations work for his own benefit while the rest of us were in the dark concerning his true identity!' she promptly accused.

'Oh, of course not!' he dissented in sudden impatience. 'As far as I'm aware, he never even mentioned the Southern Cross mine, let alone tried to persuade anyone they should be in favour of any new venture involved with it. He simply thought it wouldn't go amiss if he stayed around for a while in order to see just what the general feeling about it was . . . just in case.'

Kendra pursed her lips thoughtfully, turning back to the stove to attend to cooking their breakfasts once more. She couldn't quite decide whether she was as ready as Darby evidently had been to accept the explanation as the truth or not. Or maybe she was simply reluctant to because it only underlined how justified Rogan's anger had been in the face of her derogatory indictments, she brooded glumly.

Behind her, Darby continued wryly. 'In any event, if you want further proof that it wasn't my knowledge of the area or even my gold—that is, if the Good Cheer does eventually produce some,' he inserted graphically, 'that Rogan was most interested in, then I can supply that myself, because I'd begun to suspect long before last night that it wasn't so much to do with what came out of them, as the mines themselves.'

Hastily transferring the thankfully now cooked food on to plates which she deposited on the table—at least now she wouldn't have to keep turning back and forth all the time—Kendra seated herself across the table from him. 'I don't follow you.' She frowned.

'That's probably due to you always having been more anxious to provoke than anything else, otherwise you too—although once again I'm still somewhat surprised that you didn't—may have realised he wasn't quite what he appeared, or we, you especially, assumed him to be,' he began with a bantering smile that was repaid with an eloquent scowl of exasperation. 'Because you see, although I guess you could say that on the one hand Rogan's a part-time prospector by trade, on the other it would appear that, by profession, he's something else again.' He paused meaningfully. And deliberately! suspected Kendra with a fulminating intake of breath. 'A mining engineer, no less.'

Kendra dropped her knife and fork with a clatter. 'But he can't be! He's lived all his life way out in the bush! Or so he said,' she concluded explicitly.

'And out in that bush—with only week-old newspapers, if you're lucky, no radio and no television—there are lots of long nights most suitable for studying correspondence courses,' Darby reminded no less significantly. 'Moreover, as I just mentioned, I'd already begun to suspect something of the kind myself as a result of the more technical type of questions he mainly asked.'

As he had with her also, Kendra nodded meditatively to herself, recalling now how it had been the stacks and the poppetheads, the machinery, the kind of shafts utilised that had occupied Rogan's attention longest and prompted most of his queries the day of their tour. Following on that, she also remembered him claiming on more than one occasion that he had never allowed prospecting to completely rule his life either.

All in all, it appeared there had been quite a few clues she had missed due to her efforts to disparage his supposed occupation, and him with it, and solely because she had been so unwilling to admit, even to herself, that the real reason his presence had disturbed her to such a degree was because he had attracted her like no other man ever had before! Only now it was too late to do anything about it.

Sighing dejectedly, she lifted her eyes to Darby's, her soft mouth forming into rueful lines. 'I guess I really made a muck up of this one, didn't I?'

'Mmm, unfortunately, I think you did,' came the unexpectedly heavy concurrence that had her making her own deduction.

'And you think I should apologise.'

'Don't you consider one's due?'

'I—I suppose so,' she shrugged deprecatingly, dreading the thought. Then in a firmer tone, 'Not that I really consider it to have been all my fault, just the same. If people purposely represent themselves as something they're not, they must expect to arouse suspicions when the truth's uncovered.'

'Even though they may have had a perfectly legitimate reason, but which they're flatly denied the opportunity to disclose?' Darby raised an expressive brow.

'I—well—he wasn't exactly pleasant to me either last night, you know,' Kendra half complained, half denounced. 'Besides, if you thought I was so in the wrong, then, why did you let him move out? Why didn't you over-ride my orders instead?'

'I tried to, believe me!' he owned with a short laugh. 'But I'm afraid Rogan definitely wasn't having any of it. Whatever happened between the two of you must really have been the last straw as far as he was concerned. My God, it was almost possible to feel the explosive tension surrounding him afterwards, and with someone's who's usually so even-tempered and easy to get along with that's really something to experience, I can tell you!' He halted briefly. 'In fact, judging by Curry's manner, I don't even think he'd ever seen Rogan in such a mood either.'

'I see,' she acknowledged with a somewhat sickly gulp. It hardly augured well for making an apology. 'So where did they go? To the Searles' hotel?'

'Uh-huh.'

'Oh, well, at least that will have put Genevieve over the moon,' she quipped in falsely flippant tones, doing her best to overcome the feeling of grinding, desolating jealousy the thought engendered. It would also make it doubly hard, of course, just to separate that girl from Rogan in order to deliver her apology. One thing was for certain, though. There was no way she would be making it in front of Genevieve!

Darby, who had been displaying his normal healthy appetite throughout their conversation, unlike his sister who had been pushing her food around her plate more often than eating it, swallowed his latest mouthful and shrugged.

'You've no one but yourself to blame if she is.'

A remark that had Kendra glancing at him swiftly, covertly. Oh Lord, he hadn't somehow deduced how she really felt about Rogan, had he? With a fast beating heart she forced a note of careless insouciance into her voice.

'And why should I blame myself for that? It matters little to me where Rogan stays. I was merely commenting on Genevieve's undoubted reaction, that's all.' And in a hopefully more diverting vein, 'Although I suppose even her pleasure is likely to be short-lived, in any case, for now that his father's arrived I expect they'll both be leaving before too long, won't they?' An overwhelmingly dispiriting thought she tried valiantly to ignore.

'Some time this coming weekend, I think.' Darby nodded. 'I gather all the work that's been taking place out at the camp will be just about concluded by then. Although if everything goes according to plan, I guess we can expect to see Rogan, at least, back here again in the not too-distant future.'

That was a probability Kendra hadn't given the slightest consideration to, and her stomach constricted tightly in response to it having been brought to her notice. As much as the idea of not seeing Rogan sent waves of despair surging over her, conversely, she felt it would be even worse to constantly be seeing him around town, and yet all the while be aware there was absolutely no hope of there ever being anything between them. At least if he was out of sight there was a chance, however small, that she might also be able to put him out of her mind.

Partly for her own protection, and partly in order not to appear to have altered her stand too much, she therefore proposed in something of a nervous rush, 'None the less, you won't be suggesting he moves in here again if he does return, I trust?'

'Well—I . . .' Darby groaned hesitantly, and had her immediately fearing the worst. He gave a heaved sigh. 'You really dislike him that much?'

Kendra hunched a diffident, slender shoulder, and chose her words carefully. 'I wouldn't precisely say it's dislike, but more a—umm—clash of personalities,' she parried. To have claimed to dislike someone so damned handsome, not to mention engaging, she thought could have been just a little too much to expect anyone to believe. Luckily, another helpfully supporting remembrance ensued. 'In any case, it's not just me. Last night *he* also saw fit to advocate in no uncertain terms that I should stay out of *his* way in future too.'

'Then I guess that settles it, doesn't it?' He really had little choice but to accede, though with just enough of a disappointed nuance in his voice to bring a slight frown to his sister's forehead.

She couldn't quite make out just why he should apparently feel dissatisfied because of her falling out with Rogan. Admittedly, right from the beginning he had seemed to want her to like him, what with all his urgings to give the man a fair go, and so forth, and even his arranging for her to show Rogan over the town instead of himself.

At the time she had supposed it was just his way of wanting her to extend the same hospitality he had, but now she was starting to wonder if perhaps there couldn't have been another less obvious reason after all. But what? That was the question, of course. However, when absolutely nothing came to mind after a few deeply contemplative moments, she contrarily began to think she was maybe trying to read things that weren't there at all and, dismissing the notion altogether, gave up pretending to be interested in eating any more of her breakfast and pushed away from the table.

'So what would you like on your sandwiches today? Anything in particular?' she asked over her shoulder as she made for the fridge, reverting to the more mundane. She always provided him with a cut lunch when he was working out on his lease.

'Oh—er—nothing, thanks. As it happens, I won't be needing anything at all today,' he relayed, rising to his feet and taking his plate over to the sink. 'I'll be lunching at the hotel, as I've arranged to show Rogan . . .' a brief pause during which his lips twisted crookedly, 'now that you've—umm—relieved him of his duties, and Curry over the Good Cheer this morning.'

'Oh,' Kendra acknowledged quietly, and moving away from the fridge started clearing the table instead. 'Will you also be having dinner up there, then?'

'Uh-uh.' Darby smiled briefly and then hesitated before divulging, 'Actually, Vivian's invited me to dinner this evening. Although you're welcome to come as well, naturally, if you'd like to,' he added quickly.

An offer that was declined with a faint answering smile and a shake of the head. 'No, I think I'll just have a quiet evening at home,' she declared.

For one thing, she didn't want to intrude, because although she knew Vivian would have made her welcome, ever since Rogan had suggested there may have been more than just friendliness between her brother and his friend's widow, she had indeed been watching them more closely, and to her astonishment had eventually been forced into acceding that maybe he was right. Something of a more affectionate nature had developed between them. Nevertheless, as neither of them appeared to want to make it public as yet, although Kendra couldn't fathom why ever not, she had respected their evident wishes and not mentioned it either, even in a teasing fashion to Darby.

'Well, if you should change your mind . . .' He now eyed her implicitly, thoughtfully giving her the opportunity to reconsider if she cared to.

'I'll know where to join you,' she finished for him with a wry half laugh and a fond look.

He really was a love in lots of ways, she mused sentimentally. Unfailingly good-natured and good-humoured, kind, always willing to do a good turn, and prepared to do his utmost to comply with any request made of him. Provided that didn't include giving up his mining or his occasionally overenthusiastic drinking sprees with his mates, of course, the rueful amendment followed. She also didn't imagine there were many men who would be so well-disposed as to invite their sister along on what was ostensibly a date either.

Presently, after Darby had left to meet Rogan and Curry, and Kendra had opened the store for another day's trading, her thoughts tended to become introspective again. Only on this occasion they weren't centred on her brother, but on Rogan, as she discovered just how much of a gap his departure seemed to have created. It was incredible really that within such a relatively short time he should have been able to stamp his mark so indelibly on the place, but in spite of all her efforts to dispel the thought, it adamantly refused to budge.

She missed him, missed him terribly, and not only his strength that had made such light work of the larger items that needed shifting, but for many other reasons as well. She missed his deep laughter when something amusing had occurred, his company regardless of how provoking it may have been at times, his resonant voice, the lazy way those smoky-green eyes of his had had of looking at her, even his easy manner of dealing with the customers. As they did too, apparently, if their reactions on finding him absent were anything to judge by, she deduced as the day wore—or dragged—on.

As well, the fact that it was also one of the slackest days she could ever remember was probably a prime factor in what made his loss so very much more noticeable than it might otherwise have been, but at least that lack of clientele did allow her to reach the impulsive decision to close the store a good deal earlier than usual that afternoon, especially when coupled with another significant occurrence.

She had been standing just by the front door at the time, absently viewing the sun-dried scene across the road—the bare tailings heaps that reflected the heat

back with such ferocity; the bloodwood and ironbark
trees interspersed between them, their olive-coloured
leaves drooping downwards like all species of
eucalyptus, and always with their edges facing the sun
in order to conserve moisture; the cooler blue tinge
to the hills beyond Duffey's Peak. Then suddenly a
vehicle had sped across her line of vision, the driver
waving and calling out a greeting on seeing her, which
she had automatically returned before realisation of
the incident's import struck her a minute or so later.
Good lord, Rex Thorley, Genevieve's supposedly
fiancé-to-be, was back!

After that, her next thought had been to speculate
with uncharacteristic maliciousness as to just how the
redhead was going to extricate herself from such an
awkward, not to say possibly eruptive, situation when
Rex and Rogan came face to face. But almost
immediately another had ensued involving herself, and
in that regard it began to seem if Rex's return could
have been quite fortuitous. For no matter what the
eventual outcome, it would surely separate Genevieve
from Rogan for a while at least, and thereby provide
herself with the opportunity she required, however
reluctantly, to make her apology to Rogan in private.
The idea that Genevieve might actually be tempted to
show Rex the door altogether didn't occur to her.
After all, they had been going together for some time,
and as the other girl had once implied, in a town the
size of Goldfield one didn't deliberately create bad
feeling if it could possibly be avoided.

So it was that within twenty minutes of having seen
Rex, Kendra was also setting off up the street in the
same direction, although with markedly less enthusiasm. There was no time like the present, she kept
repeating in order to convince herself, so if an apology
had to be made it was better to do so as soon as

possible and then she could go about putting the whole perturbing episode behind her. Well, at least as much as she would ever be able to, she modified honestly, if somewhat disconsolately.

It wasn't until she had almost reached the hotel, though, that she abruptly recalled Darby saying he'd arranged to show both Rogan and his father over his mine that day, and momentarily she stopped, berating herself for having forgotten and rubbing the palms of her hands, which had become increasingly damp during her walk, down the sides of her jeans. Tempted to take the easy way out and simply return home, Kendra hovered uncertainly where she was for a second or two, knowing she should check to see if they had returned all the same, and then the matter was taken out of her hands altogether by Curran Faulkner suddenly appearing in the doorway.

'Kendra! This is a pleasant surprise.' He smiled on seeing her, and which she considered very generous of him under the circumstances. He took a few steps forward, his brows lifting. 'You're looking for Darby, are you?'

Swallowing hard, she shook her head. 'No, I—I was wanting a word with—with Rogan if possible, actually, and—and to apologise to you for my behaviour last night really,' she just managed to stammer embarrassedly, but believing him to be entitled to that much at least. 'I'm afraid you didn't receive a very polite reception and—and I'm sorry.'

'That's all right, love, I understand.' Curry smiled again, charitably. 'But you go on up if you want to see Rogan. We're just having a drink on the side balcony. Perhaps you'd like one too, eh?' His brown eyes widened enquiringly. 'I just came down for some refills.'

'Oh—er—not for me, thank you,' she refused

awkwardly, her gaze involuntarily straying to the balcony above as she hesitated over his first suggestion also.

As if sensing her reluctance, he promptly hazarded in kindly tones, 'Or would you prefer to speak to him down here?' On receiving a self-conscious and slightly stilted nod, he was already turning back towards the door as he advised, 'You just wait here, then, and I'll let him know.' And was gone before she could voice her gratitude.

While she waited, Kendra moved nervously from one foot to the other, trying to formulate in her mind what she would say, and then the sound of feet on the wooden balcony above had her looking upwards to see Rogan leaning negligently against the intricately designed, wrought-iron railing.

'You've something to say to me, I understand,' he said coolly.

She nodded uncomfortably. Noting even from that distance that the eyes which had been so brilliantly green the night before were now pure grey, the lazy lights normally visible therein nowhere in evidence today. It was hardly an auspicious omen.

'Well?' came the equally chilly but increasingly impatient prompting.

Kendra bit at her lip in despair. Not that she supposed he should, but he certainly wasn't making it any easier. It wasn't something one wanted to have to shout so everyone could hear. With her thickly lashed eyes shadowing with unwitting reproach, she executed a deprecating shrug.

'It doesn't matter, it wasn't urgent. It can wait until some other time,' she declared on a strained note. 'I— I'm sorry to have bothered you.' She about-faced rapidly and started hurrying down the hill again.

'Kendra!' Rogan immediately called, half in exasperation, half in command, but she didn't even slow as she ignored it, her eyes suddenly blurring with welling tears.

Oh, what a hideous mess she had made of everything, she choked miserably. If only she had just accepted him as Darby had then maybe none of this would have happened. But no, she'd been too intent on roasting him at every turn and attempting to prove her own theories. Apparently horribly incorrect ones, at that!

She was some distance down the street when an unanticipated and inflexible hand on her shoulder whirled her around, gasping in surprise, to face Rogan's intimidating figure and somewhat less than patient countenance.

'Okay, so just what was that all in aid of?' he demanded roughly.

Without having been given the chance to brush away her tell-tale tears, Kendra averted her still awash gaze quickly, defensively. 'I said it didn't matter. Th-that it could wait until some other time,' she faltered evasively.

'Mmm, I know what you said. Now I want to know why!' A hand beneath her chin ensured she couldn't avoid his hard, probing scrutiny any longer. A survey that unexpectedly lost some of its harshness on observing what she had so wanted to hide, and had him exhaling heavily. 'I'm sorry if I was the cause of that.'

Terrified he might also guess just why he had the power to make her dissolve into such inconsolable tears, she frantically sought to protect herself with a denial of faked indifference. 'Oh, don't worry, you weren't! It was simply a result of—of walking into the full glare of the sun, that's all. I obviously should have worn my dark glasses.'

Rogan stifled a savage expletive, his grip on her jaw tightening imperceptibly. 'That isn't all that's obvious!' he clipped out with barely suppressed anger, and had her holding her breath in fear of his meaning. 'But then, I guess anticipating you being anything *but* intransigent really would be expecting too much, wouldn't it?'

Uncomplimentary though the remark was, Kendra still sagged with relief. 'In that case, you won't be wanting the apology you undoubtedly weren't expecting either, and evidently couldn't have cared less about receiving anyway!' The gibing words spilled out uncontrollably in her now less apprehensive state.

'Meaning, that was why you wanted to speak to me?' He uttered a short, unamused laugh. 'You're right! That that might be the reason didn't ever occur to me! So who put you up to it . . . Darby?'

'No!' she protested resentfully, knocking his hand away in a furious movement that provided the desired physical outlet for her rising emotions. 'Although I can see it was a complete waste of time in view of your . . .'

'Then waste a bit more . . . as I'm having to do since I was misguided enough to come after you in the first place!' Rogan cut her off to instruct with a bite.

'But which was probably only because I didn't immediately jump to obey the minute you called out to me!'

For the space of a few seconds Rogan's eyes narrowed dangerously. 'While your supposed apology would appear to be nothing more than an excuse to start another confrontation!' he denounced in an ominously grating voice before turning on his heel and heading back to the hotel.

With his departure, Kendra's heightened feelings promptly plunged downwards once more. Oh God, she'd done it again! Why couldn't she have just accepted that he *had* come after her, when all was said and done, and left it at that?

'Rogan!' It was she who was left to call anxiously after him now. And when he showed no signs of heeding, to following him with quickening steps. 'Rogan ... please!' She reached out a tentative hand to catch at his arm when she drew alongside him, only to withdraw it again before actually doing so. 'I—I'm sorry, honestly I am. Won't you please stop for a moment?'

For the first time he acknowledged she was even there, although he still didn't come to a halt. He merely flicked her a caustically expressive glance and quizzed, 'What for? Another altercation?'

'No! So I can ...' She broke off in order to entreat on an increasingly imploring note, 'Rogan, *please*! I can't talk to you while I'm almost running!' His long legs were outpacing hers all too easily. 'And whether you believe it or not, it was my intention t-to apologise.' A slight break made an appearance in her voice.

Now he stopped, but with such abruptness that Kendra almost cannoned into him. 'So why didn't you?' he demanded curtly.

'I meant to at the hotel, but when you didn't come down ...' She paused, hunching a deprecating shoulder. 'Well, I—I didn't want to shout it up to the balcony.'

'Nor even say it at all afterwards, apparently!' His tone was as uncompromising as ever.

'I've already apologised f-for that,' she reminded unsteadily. 'But it's very difficult to say sorry to someone who—who's ...'

'Inconsiderately disproved your prejudiced theories?'

'No! That has nothing to do with it. Although I—I'm still entitled to my opinion, even if it doesn't tally with yours.'

'Obdurate to the end, huh?'

Kendra forbore to answer directly. She couldn't afford to have him delving into her reasoning too deeply. Instead, she simply countered with a pensive sigh, 'So who's looking for another argument now?'

'Hmm . . .' Fleetingly, Rogan's expression took on a ruefully humorous aspect, and then it was gone again as he granted impassively, 'Okay, the floor's all yours.'

Thankful for that at least, Kendra nodded, but still kept her eyes downcast as she agitatedly sought the right words. All her previously conceived phrases had long since fled. 'Yes—well—I just wanted to say I was sorry for—for the way I reacted to your father's disclosures last night, and for having accused you of . . .' she swallowed painfully, 'the things I did,' she just managed to get out at length. Her troubled blue eyes flickered upwards briefly. 'I now know differently and—and I apologise for having immediately suspected the worse.'

'Accused me of the worst would be more like it, wouldn't it?' Sardonically.

She took a long, ragged breath and nodded. 'I'm sorry.'

Rogan was silent for a moment, and then, 'So how come Darby was able to convince you,' a fair deduction as to who had converted her thinking, 'when I couldn't?'

'You didn't try to,' she disclaimed, shooting another swift glance at his dishearteningly remote features. 'You just . . . lost your temper and retaliated with s-some accusations of your own, and the recommendation that I—I keep out of your way in future.'

'I wonder why!' He half laughed abrasively. 'Not that you seem to have paid much attention to that last direction, in any case.'

Kendra thought that was more than a little unfair considering the circumstances that had prompted her to seek him out, but at the same time it also made it all too clear that, her apology notwithstanding, he found her presence unwanted and unwelcome.

'I'm sorry,' she said once more in a strained whisper, her heart shrivelling. 'I'll do my utmost to see it doesn't happen again.'

'That could be best,' Rogan had no compunction in agreeing on a rough-edged note, although without immediately making a move to leave.

That was left to Kendra, who did so rapidly while she was still possessed of some modicum of feigned unconcern. 'Yes,' she got out past the lump in her throat and took to her heels before another word could be said. She only wanted the solitude and safety of her home which would hopefully provide solace for her torn and anguished spirit.

However, it appeared not even that was to be allowed her, for memories of Rogan were everywhere. Memories she wanted desperately to discard, and yet waywardly wanted to retain and treasure too. It was a self-defeating situation of torment which, consequently, had her greeting Mike Warden's arrival a short time later with a relief she hadn't expected to feel on having her seclusion disturbed when she had first made it back to the house.

'Hi! How come the store's closed?' was his first surprised question on entering the kitchen and casually taking a seat at the table. 'At first I thought you must have been out of town for the day.'

Kendra partly turned away, ostensibly occupied in pouring him a mug of coffee. Mike always drank it in preference to tea. 'No, I simply decided to give myself an early mark, that's all,' she declared in what she hoped was a suitably offhand manner.

To her relief he accepted the explanation without question, but went on to speculate, 'In order to get things back to normal here, I suppose? I heard that Faulkner moved out and into the hotel last night.'

It came as no surprise to her that he knew. In such a small town very little occurred that everyone didn't know about. 'That's right,' she acceded, carefully nonchalant, and setting the mug before him prior to taking a seat herself. 'His father arrived so they— umm—both booked into the hotel. I believe they'll be leaving altogether this weekend, in any event.'

'Mmm, I heard that as well,' Mike revealed in musing tones. 'I also understand Faulkner isn't exactly the pauper we all took him to be either.'

'Far from it, it would seem in fact!' She attempted to laugh, but it had too brittle a sound to it to be natural.

Her companion didn't appear to notice, however. 'That must have come as something of a shock, to you especially,' he contended.

'Implying?' Kendra stiffened warily.

'With regard to your feelings concerning prospectors, naturally!' he elucidated, looking at her askance. 'What did you think I was implying?'

'Oh, nothing in particular, I—I just wasn't sure, that's all,' she excused somewhat lamely.

Once again Mike seemed to be too preoccupied with his own train of thought for it to register. 'Yes, well, I can't say it didn't shake me a bit also, discovering he wasn't exactly penniless, and I don't mind admitting that I wasn't at all sorry to learn he'd moved out of here,' he owned in wry accents.

'From your remarks the night you first met him, I guess that doesn't altogether amaze me,' she quipped drily, remembering his abrupt loss of self-confidence and his ensuing attitude.

'So who'd blame me?' His lips twisted expressively. 'With that macho look about him,' grudgingly conceded, '. . . among other things, he's not the sort of feller any guy wants staying in the same house as his girlfriend. Then to find out he also has money to go with it, well . . .' He reached over to clasp one of her hands in his, his eyes darkening. 'Why wouldn't I be edgy thinking he might steal you away from me?'

Momentarily, Kendra sat staring at him helplessly, unsure just what to say. For a start, she was at something of a loss to see how she could be stolen away when she had never actually given him cause to believe she was his in the first place. More relevantly, of course, how on earth was she to convince him there never had been any likelihood of Rogan coming between them without giving him the impression she least wanted to create—that of her already having considered him as the sole man in her life. Deciding finally that she had to at least say *something*, and soon, she began by forcing out an ironic laugh.

'Insomuch as Rogan and I were rarely in accord over anything, I can assure you there was very little chance of him disrupting any *friendly*,' purposely stressed, 'relationship you and I might have.'

'Friendly?' Mike uttered a slightly scoffing laugh. 'That's rather an insipid way of describing what we've got going between us, isn't it?'

Unobtrusively withdrawing her hand from his, Kendra sucked in a bolstering breath and thought inconsequentially that it must be her day for apologies as she half smiled regretfully. 'I'm sorry, Mike, but that *is* how I think of it. How I've always thought of it.' Her eyes held his resolutely. 'Neither am I aware of ever having given you reason to believe otherwise.'

'Except by always accepting my invitations to go out, of course!' he retorted hotly. Cooling down again quickly, he went on to exhort, 'Kendra, you can't mean it! You know how much we've enjoyed being together . . . how I've always included you in my plans for the future. I've certainly made no secret of how I feel about you. So how you can now claim it to have been mere friendship is beyond me!' A touch of resentment began filtering into his voice.

Kendra sighed uncomfortably, reluctant to hurt his feelings, but simultaneously aware she couldn't permit him to continue thinking she reciprocated those feelings. 'Because, I'm sorry, that's all it has been for me,' she advised in contrite tones. 'We have had some good times together, I know, and I have enjoyed your company, but I'm afraid that's all it was on my part . . . friendly enjoyment. Nothing of a more serious nature.' She hesitated. 'As—as I hoped you would realise when I always avoided committing myself to anything of that kind.'

'I see.' His jaw tightened grimly. 'In other words, I've just been wasting my time, have I?' He paused. 'While you've simply been making use of me!'

'I suppose you could see it in that light if you wanted to, although that certainly wasn't my intention,' she defended gravely.

'Then why in God's name . . .!' He broke off, running a hand around his neck distractedly. 'Oh, Kendra, you really know how to effectively bring someone down to size, don't you? I had such plans for us, too. Which, I might point out, you sure didn't appear to object to when I mentioned them either!' Again his voice became imbued with recrimination. Abruptly, his eyes narrowed. 'Only now have you seen fit to say anything! Since Rogan Faulkner's arrival in

town! Which wouldn't have anything to do with it by
any chance, I suppose?' Sarcasm uppermost now.

'None whatsoever!' Kendra was thankful to be able
to deny truthfully.

Mike's suspicious expression didn't alter by so
much as a fraction, however. 'You expect me to
believe that?'

'If you have the slightest interest in the truth, yes!'
Kendra's own feelings started to become a little
heated.

'Hah!' His exclamation was part scornfully, part
ironically made. 'Since I've no real proof to the
contrary, I guess I don't have much option but to
believe you, do I?' he allowed with tangible reluctance.

'Well, *thank you*!' Her answer was acidly emphas-
ised. 'Your magnanimity is positively overpowering,
particularly when I would have thought that even you
couldn't have missed noticing that it's been Genevieve
who's been keeping him well and truly occupied since
he arrived . . . not me!'

'It was in this house that he was still living, though,
wasn't it?'

'So?' Her eyes sparkled militantly.

'So who knows what went on here when Genevieve
wasn't with him!'

'Insinuating, that I generously made myself available—and in the most promiscuous sense, presumably—to fill in his hours away from her, is that it?'
she surmised in irate indignation. 'My, that was the
ultimate in hospitality, considering how at odds we
were over just about everything else while he was
here!' Sharply mocking.

'Well, how was I . . .' Mike came to a stop after his
first few forceful words, releasing a heavy breath. 'Oh,
hell! I'm sorry. I don't know what's got into me. I
guess I just wanted to believe, for my own benefit at

least, that someone else was the cause of your attitude.'

With his change in manner, so did Kendra's alter as well. To one of reconciliation as she put forward softly, 'I would hope that we can still remain friends, none the less.'

'Since that's apparently all there is on offer, do I have much choice?' he quipped, not totally with humour, as he rose to his feet and started for the door. 'Not that there's any reason to suppose I won't recover, of course, even though it is a bit deflating at the moment.' His usual self-confidence began re-asserting itself. And looking back over his shoulder, 'You still want me to take you to the dance on Saturday?'

'I would, if you're also agreeable.'

'Okay.' He shrugged with a casualness that, whether feigned or not at present, had Kendra strongly suspecting it wouldn't take him very long at all to restore his injured pride, and most likely with some other, more appreciative female. 'I'll be down about seven-thirty, then,' he added, putting out a hand to push open the screen door, only to find it already swinging away from him by virtue of Darby preparing to enter.

'Oh, g'day,' said the older man somewhat absently as he passed into the room. 'You're just leaving, are you?'

'Yeah.' Mike's mouth curved wryly. 'I figured it was about time.'

'What did he mean by that?' frowned Darby once Mike had departed. 'You've had a blue with him too, have you?'

'Not really,' Kendra refuted a little huffily, taking his obvious inference amiss. 'More a clearing up of a misunderstanding, as it so happens.'

'Like . . .?' His expression suddenly became more intent.

She grimaced. 'Like, informing him I wasn't interested in making our relationship a permanent one.'

'Because you've got someone else in mind?'

Knowing the answer she only wished she could give to that was out of the question had her retorting testily. 'Oh, of course not! How in blazes could I have? There's hardly what you would call an unlimited choice in Goldfield, and since none of the others have ever particularly interested me anyway . . .' She pulled another eloquent face.

Darby threw up his hands in mock surrender. 'It was only a thought.' He hesitated briefly. 'See, I told you you could do worse than turn your eye in Rogan's direction.'

So he had, but at the moment she couldn't quite grasp what he was getting at, or even why he had brought the matter up in view of the way things stood. 'Because he turned out to be well-heeled instead of impecunious, you mean?' she therefore questioned dubiously.

'Not especially.' He shrugged, and folding his arms across his chest as he leant back against a cupboard, eyed her half wryly, half contemplatively. 'You know, I really did expect you to like him, though, even before we found out about that.' He expelled a long breath. 'To be honest, for a while there I was even hoping something might eventuate between the two of you, in fact.'

'Oh?' Kendra's finely arching brows peaked in surprise, and then promptly lowered to a frown as she recalled the manner in which he had indeed always seemed to be recommending Rogan to her. She wished she had paid more attention to his urgings now, of course, but at the same time she still felt the need to puzzle, 'For any particular reason?'

Darby cleared his throat, looking strangely discomfited. 'I—well—just that right from our first meeting, I don't know why, but I simply felt he'd be a—a good husband for you.'

'You were *matchmaking*?' she burst out in disbelief, not knowing whether to laugh or fume. 'And that's why you offered him work in the store? Oh, Darby, how could you?' She sank on to a seat at the table to regard him with sardonic eyes. 'Are you that anxious to get me out of your hair?'

'No! No, of course not!' He swiftly took the chair around the corner of the table from her, adding earnestly, 'You must know that's not true! Besides, this is your home as much as mine, so you've a perfect right to be here. It was just that . . . well, in spite of my teasing you about Mike being so keen, I did suspect you may not have been as eager—you see, my thoughts don't always only revolve around the mine,' he inserted on a chaffing note, 'so I thought I could maybe do you a favour by introducing you to someone I at least considered more likely to—er—capture your fancy.' There was a slight pause during which he executed a rueful smile. 'Though I must admit it could possibly have been the drink I'd consumed that prompted the idea, and had me going through with it.'

'Hmm . . .' She slanted him an oblique glance, and then abruptly gasped. 'Oh, God, you didn't tell Rogan that was why you were hiring him, did you?' That gave rise to too many mortifying thoughts to even contemplate!

'No, no!' He hastened to set her mind at ease. 'I hadn't lost my wits to *that* extent. In any case, I doubt he would have agreed if I had. He always strikes me as the kind to do the leading, not to being led.'

Kendra nodded. Despite Rogan's customary easy-going nature, there still had always been something about him that proclaimed he would never be anything else but his own man.

'Well, I apologise for foiling your plans,' she declared with protective flippacy. 'So you'll just have to resign yourself to putting up with me for a while longer, I'm afraid. Maybe you should have told me what you had in the back of your devious little mind.' She started to leave her chair again in order to begin preparing dinner.

'Lord, no!' Darby rolled his eyes skywards significantly. 'That probably would have been worse than telling Rogan.' He caught at her arm to forestall her leaving the table, going on to instruct in sobering tones, 'No, forget that for the time being. I've something important I want to tell you. And you may even need one of these while I'm doing it.' Giving a slightly ragged laugh he tossed his cigarettes and lighter on to the table.

A sudden disquiet had Kendra regaining her seat without question and making use of the cigarettes provided. Not since their parents' deaths could she remember seeing Darby look quite so serious—reminding her of his seeming preoccupation when he first returned—and that paired to that rather uneasy laugh he'd just uttered had her drawing on her cigarette nervously.

'Yes?' her prompting was tautly made.

Darby finished applying a flame to the tip of his own cigarette and half smiled. If it was intended to be encouraging his sister could have told him it had failed. 'Well, as you know, I showed Rogan and Curry over the Good Cheer today,' he began slowly, as if selecting his words with great care. 'And afterwards we had quite a talk about it at the hotel.'

'Go on,' she pressed in wary accents when a short lull ensued.

'Umm—you wouldn't realise it, of course, but if they're granted all the leases they plan to apply for—and to date there's no reason to believe they won't be as they've gone into it pretty thoroughly, detailing anticipated ways of disposing of waste, likely environmental impact, proposed rehabilitation methods, etcetera—then one of their boundaries will adjoin my lease.'

Kendra's stomach constricted, her brows drawing into a suspicious line. 'And?' she fairly grated.

'It's certainly a huge area they'll be covering,' Darby mused appreciatively—and quite immaterially to his sister's mind, even if it did abruptly bring home to her just how large a venture it was likely to be—as he blew a stream of smoke ceilingwards.

'So why not just claim the whole damned town as well and be done with it?' she sniped. Then reiterated stonily, 'And?'

'Yes, well, for an open-cut operation you naturally require a few square miles at least, but it's a far better method of ensuring whatever's there is actually found,' he continued in the same vein as before.

He was deliberately avoiding the issue! seethed Kendra, her already mounting suspicions multiplying rapidly. 'Okay, Darby, so just what is it that you evidently feel I should know, but are just as obviously reluctant to reveal?' she demanded causstically. 'Was I right, after all, in accusing Rogan of being underhanded? Is that it? Have you suddenly discovered he's somehow managed to find a way to ride roughshod over you, only you don't want to admit as much? Is that it, Darby? Is it?'

'No, it's not!' There was no equivocation in his manner now as he shot her a censuring glance. 'But when the mere mention of the size and location of their leases generates a reaction like that—as disappointingly predictable as it was—why would I attempt to broach the subject with anything *but* extreme reluctance?' Pausing, he shook his head incredulously. 'For crying out loud, Kendra, only this morning you were conceding you'd been wrong in mistaking Rogan's motives, and yet here you are jumping to the same erroneous conclusions all over again! What in heaven's name have you got against the man?'

She didn't answer that, but countered fiercely in lieu, 'Well, what did you expect me to think with all the hedging you were doing? And if he is so blameless, why all the evasion in the first place?'

'Because on taking into account your fiery attitude to the subject I couldn't even be certain there wouldn't be an identical explosion on your hearing what *I've* done this afternoon!'

'What *you've* done?' Astonishment had her staring at him blankly. Followed by an uncontrollably wary, 'At whose instigation?'

'Oh, hell, not again!' Darby heaved an exasperated sigh and levelled a reproving look at her. 'But as it so happens, it was at *my own* instigation. I do sometimes manage to stumble upon an idea or two without any outside help—meaning Rogan on this occasion, for your information—even though you do apparently believe it utterly improbable.' A current of satirical mockery ran through his words.

Abashed, Kendra felt her cheeks warm discomfitedly. 'I'm sorry,' she apologised, and took a deep bracing draw on her cigarette. 'So what did *you* do this afternoon, then?'

'First, I should perhaps explain that their information all points to what I've been claiming for years...that there is gold, and in quantity too, in the vicinity of the Good Cheer.' He gave an oblique grin. 'Even if neither Dad nor I were ever able to locate it.'

This time Kendra didn't comment, but waited, if not patiently then at least prudently, for him to continue.

'And that being the case, I thought the matter over for a while—gauging whether there was any guarantee that I'd find it by my methods even so, the time it would take if I did, that sort of thing—and on impulse ... rushed in where angels fear to tread,' he concluded on a whimsical half laugh, and in something of a hurry.

Kendra inhaled apprehensively. 'Meaning?' she just had to ask now.

'I offered them the Good Cheer in exchange for a proportionate percentage of the whole operation.'

Momentarily, the full implication of what he was saying didn't register with her as her thoughts all concentrated on one aspect. 'B-but the mine's always been your whole life!' she exclaimed.

'Well—yes,' he granted, and to her amazement, proceeded to evade her gaze somewhat self-consciously. 'However, circumstances can change and—and in this instance I felt it was too good an opportunity to let pass. Even if only to—to finally have my theories regarding the mine proved correct.'

A spur-of-the-moment addition that last remark, suspected Kendra immediately as a result of the unsettled manner in which it had been delivered. Twin creases made an appearance between her brows. 'So precisely which circumstances are you referring to? *Just* the Faulkners' intended operations here?'

Darby drew on his cigarette quickly and hunched a deprecating shoulder. 'I—well—no, not exactly. The work does become harder as a man gets older,' making it sound as he was fifty-two instead of thirty-two, noted his sister drily, 'and—and there are other considerations, naturally.'

'Such as?' she questioned doggedly. He wasn't going to get out of it that easily. Come what may she meant to discover just expressly why he had made such an astonishing and singularly uncharacteristic decision.

'Oh—er—as you've said many times in the past, the always present possibility of accidents, the—umm—fact that I'm never here when a hand is needed with the heavy stuff in the store, the little return the mine is providing at present for the amount of time and effort expended on it, the number of hours I spend out there, and so forth,' he recounted parrot fashion.

None of which ever caused him to lose so much as a moment's sleep before, however! reflected his sister sardonically. So what had brought about his change of heart now? Not for a second did she believe it was solely due to the opportunity presented. All of a sudden one particular answer leapt to mind and she wondered why she hadn't thought of it before. Of course, that had to be the reason, she decided, and sent a chafing look in Darby's direction.

'You've forgotten the most important consideration of all, haven't you?' she charged on a wry note. 'Like—Vivian—for instance?'

His expression took on a decidedly sheepish cast. 'Oh! So you've guessed about that, have you?' He didn't bother to deny it.

'Mmm.' Her confirmation was expressively laconic. 'Although why you couldn't have just said that was the reason, goodness only knows!' She tilted her head to one side. 'Why all the attempted secrecy?'

Stubbing out his cigarette, Darby sighed, and to her surprise began to appear a trifle ill-at-ease once more. 'Well, it's hard to—er—explain really. We just decided it would be best if we—we kept it to ourselves for the time being, that's all.'

'Darby Onslow, that's the weakest excuse I've ever heard!' Kendra made no bones about letting him know exactly what she thought of his explanation. 'Best for what reason? And for whom? As far as I know there isn't a . . .' She came to an abrupt halt, her eyes widening in realisation as yet again her subconscious provided the answer. 'Good grief, it's the house, isn't it? If you marry, the pair of you will naturally expect to live here, but since I've been running it for so long now you think I'd be sure to step on Vivian's toes, or vice versa, if we all lived here, don't you?' Pausing, another speculation surfaced, but this one was somewhat more depressing than the others, as evidenced by her saddening demeanour as she put forward dismally, 'And is that also why you came up with the idea of matchmaking? To conveniently get me out of the way, after all?'

'No, honestly, love, I swear to you that wasn't the reason!' Darby tried to impress on her urgently. 'Oh, true, I'm not saying it wouldn't have solved the problem if it had come off—it's just a damned shame Vivian's house is owned by the Education Department or we may have been able to come to some satisfactory arrangement that way—but please believe me, that wasn't the motive I had in mind. I truly thought you'd like Rogan, and that the two of you would go well together. You've got to believe that!' The exhortation came sincerely.

Allowing herself to be convinced—not only because there *had* been the ring of truth in his voice, but because to have done otherwise would surely only have caused more distress for both of them—Kendra affected an air of insouciance.

'Well, if only you hadn't been quite so uncommunicative I could have set your mind at rest long ago. Because as it happens, if it hadn't been for wondering who would take care of the store, I've been considering broadening my horizons, so to speak, by leaving Goldfield for a while,' she announced, albeit not particularly truthfully, but at least proving she also could make impetuous decisions. The main advantage to be gained by such a course being, naturally, that it ensured she wouldn't be around when Rogan returned to supervise the establishment of the new workings. 'I thought I might try Townsville, or one of the other places on the coast. It would certainly be different to live near the sea for a time, and as a matter of fact I only had a letter from Monica Barnett,' their local postmaster's daughter, 'the other week, and by all accounts she's having a marvellous time working on one of the resort islands on the reef. I think I could take a dose of that without any trouble whatsoever,' with a determinedly enthusiastic smile. 'So if obtaining money in order to maybe build a new house played any part in your decision today, you don't have to give it another thought any more.'

'It didn't. Well, not to any appreciable degree,' Darby amended offhandedly, his glance considering as it remained fixed on her. 'But that's the first time I've ever heard you even contemplating leaving Goldfield. I always thought you said you never wanted to live anywhere but in the bush.'

'Yes, well, but as I also just said, it's only been the store that's prevented me from at least sampling how others live before this, so as I presume you'll be looking after that now that you've made this deal with the Faulkners, there seems no call for me to put off leaving any longer, and especially as it will make matters so much less complicated for you and Vivian.'

'Except that, understandably, no such agreement has actually been reached as yet,' he put in bluntly. 'When all's said and done, their concerns have only involved themselves to date, so it would be quite a deviation for them to include an outsider, and certainly not something they're likely to agree to without due deliberation.'

'In other words . . . whether the Good Cheer will be sufficiently lucrative to make it worth their while?' Kendra grimaced.

'They would hardly be good businessmen if that wasn't a telling component in their considerations, now would they?' countered Darby in dry tones.

'No, I suppose not,' she allowed grudgingly, sighing. 'And I guess it must take quite an amount of capital to start something like they're envisaging right from scratch.'

'Uh-huh!' Explicitly.

'Then in view of Rogan's earlier claims about having been dragged from camp to camp in the bush as a kid, and later having to turn his hand to anything that came along, which hardly conjures up a picture of luxury living—unless of course they were all fabrications, too,' she tartly interposed, 'just where did the money come from that enabled them to start up the same type of business in the Gulf? A loan from a bank, or something similar?'

Darby shook his head. 'No, simply one of those freakish occurrences of good fortune,' he relayed. 'It seems a great-uncle of Curry's—whom he never even knew he had—devoted his life to playing the stock market, with phenomenal success as it turned out, and on his death Curry inherited the lot as his sole relative, since his great-uncle had never had any children of his own or even ever married, if it comes to that.'

'I see,' Kendra acknowledged quietly. Then, in a purposely brightening, teasing tone, 'But which, in a roundabout fashion anyway, has enabled Vivian to succeed where I've failed for years,' once again as Rogan had predicted, came the rueful recollection, 'in getting you to give up working in that mine of yours.'

'Well, that still remains to be seen,' he cautioned.

'Although you did say their tests had indicated it could be promising?'

He grinned. 'Let's just say, I'm a little confident but extremely hopeful.'

'Then so will I be, for your sake.' She smiled back. And this time when she rose to begin preparing dinner, Darby didn't stop her.

CHAPTER SIX

FOR the remainder of the week the town was abuzz
with interest and speculation as the geologists from the
New Southern Cross Consolidated Mining Company
moved on to Darby's lease to begin conducting their
test drills. It even managed to put the bush dance that
was to be held at the School of Mines hall that
Saturday into the background, which was no mean
feat. Just about the whole of the population of
Goldfield and the surrounding district turned out for
these dances, which were held every couple of months
or so, and which would normally be the main topic of
conversation during the week preceding them.

Bush dances were always happy, lively affairs,
suitable for both adults and children alike as everyone
clapped their hands and stamped their feet to the
spirited strains of traditional bush music, provided by
an impromptu band of local players. There was old
Mick Fowler who was eighty-five if he was a day and
the last of the town's earlier miners, but who could
still remember what it had been like in its heyday
when the main street had been filled with buildings
and crowded with people, especially on Saturday
nights. Retired for many years now, Mick lived a
simple existence in the same small dwelling he had
occupied on the outskirts of town for the last sixty
years, but once he had his equally aged button-
accordion in his hands his fingers became as nimble as
ever they had been in his youth as they reproduced all
the old foot-tapping tunes with undiminished fervour.

On banjo there would be Rex Thorley's father,

Dave, whose whole family had always been encouraged
to play some musical instrument or the other, a
brother and sister of his, who also lived on properties
in the area, being the group's two fiddlers, while Rex
himself plunked out the rhythm on a tea-chest bass.
Their guitarist was a stockman who had taught
himself to play by ear, with surprising proficiency,
their pianist Genevieve Searle's mother, who although
having a preference for the classics still entered into
the mood of things with fittingly rousing accom-
paniments.

Aware that this Saturday's dance was sure to be
different, however—not only because of the presence
of the two principals of the new mining venture that
everyone seemed to be eagerly hoping would bring a
return of prosperity to the town after so many years,
but also because it was as certain to be dominated by
such talk—Kendra initially considered not attending.
But when further contemplation gradually raised the
surmise that such an absence would most likely only
create even more surprised conjecturing—drawing
attention she definitely didn't want, if not deductions
she would prefer even less—it eventually became
apparent that, reluctant or not, there was simply no
feasible excuse for her to avoid going.

Consequently, Saturday afternoon found her, as
normal for all the women thereabouts on such an
occasion, cooking sausage rolls, cakes and tarts for the
supper that would be provided during the evening's
entertainment, although with markedly less enthusiasm
than she would customarily have felt.

In fact, by the time the hour of seven arrived and
she started donning a pale apricot camisole-styled, fine
cotton blouse, and a darker paprika coloured flaring
skirt, cinched about her slim waist with a wide,
matching leather belt, and showing a length of shapely

leg above her tan sandalled feet, she was closer to a state of agitated dismay than anything else.

Just the knowledge that Rogan and his father would be leaving early the following morning, received via Darby, was enough to confuse her with feelings of despair on realising tonight would undoubtedly be the last time she would see Rogan due to her resolved plan to leave Goldfield for an extended period, not to mention converse feelings of a somewhat determined relief at the idea of not having to be constantly on her guard as a result of his wholly discomposing presence in town.

'Mike's here!' Darby called to advise as she was finishing applying a coating of coral lipstick to her curving mouth, and giving her hair a last swift brush. Kendra sighed fatalistically and made her way out to the kitchen.

Unable to completely conceal his admiration for the attractive picture she made, Mike immediately enquired in a gruff tone, 'Ready?' and began picking up the food-filled containers waiting on the table.

Nodding, Kendra turned to her brother. 'We'll see you there shortly, then.'

'Mmm, in fact I'll leave with you. I was just about on my way to collect Vivian when Mike arrived.' Opening the door, he gestured for both her and her laden companion to precede him outside.

At the front of the house they parted company, Darby heading for Vivian's, Kendra and Mike making towards the hall that stood out like a beacon at the top of the gently sloping street, its every window bright with welcoming light. Soon they were being passed by an almost continuous stream of vehicles coming from the outlying districts, filled with station owners, managers, or married stockmen, together with their families, plus many a ute loaded with single stockmen as well. All of them converging on the hall with a good deal of vocal high spirits and much laughter. Everyone always anticipated having a good time at the bush dances.

As Kendra and Mike reached the building they could just hear over the general hubbub of sound coming from inside, Frank Edgar, the caller, making the first of what would be many such invitations that night, 'Ladies and gentlemen, take your partners . . .' and before they had finished paying their entrance fees and passed from the small entry into the main hall, the first quadrille of the evening was under way.

Carefully skirting the gaily garbed dancers—the men mostly in slim-fitting moleskins, check shirts of various hues, and low-heel stock boots; their partners in just as colourful dresses and skirts—they made for one of the rooms that led off the side of the hall that had been converted into a kitchen, where Mike deposited his load before returning to watch the dancing.

Putting off the inevitable for as long as possible, Kendra stayed talking to some of the other women in the room, helping to lay out all the cups and saucers that would be required at supper time, getting out the big enamel teapots, filling bowls with sugar and jugs with milk. The latter being placed in the old fridge someone had once donated. All the cream-filled cakes and tarts were stored in there too, the night being far too warm to chance leaving them out even if only for a couple of hours.

As all the other women finally prepared to leave the room in order to participate in the evening's fun, though, Kendra was grudgingly obliged to do the same. She couldn't remain in the kitchen *all* night, that was for sure! Even Vivian, and the other more recent arrivals, were returning to the hall now.

'Swing your partners!' Frank was urging the

whirling dancers performing The Stockyards Jig that was in progress as Kendra and the others returned to the main hall, and dropping back beside Vivian, the younger girl lowered her head slightly.

'I understand congratulations are in order with regard to you and Darby,' she murmured in an aside under cover of the music and pounding feet.

Vivian nodded somewhat shyly, a faint flush mounting her cheeks. 'Mmm, Darby mentioned you'd guessed how we feel about one another.' Her blue eyes sought Kendra's a little anxiously. 'You don't mind?'

'Heavens, no!' the prompt denial was patently genuine. 'I can't think of anyone I'd rather have as my sister-in-law.'

With a partly relieved, partly grateful look, Vivian shrugged diffidently. 'I thought perhaps my having been married before, and having a son as well . . .' She spread her hands meaningfully.

Suddenly catching sight of young Jimmy following Darby like a shadow and then grinning widely in response to something her brother turned to say to him, Kendra shook her head and smiled. 'A son Darby's only too pleased to become a father to, by the look of it.'

'Yes, it is lovely that they get along so well together, isn't it?' Vivian agreed, her expression fond as her gaze also rested briefly on the pair across the hall. Then glancing at the girl beside her again, 'But Darby was also saying you're thinking of leaving Goldfield for a while.' A worried frown drew her blonde brows together. 'I do hope that's not because of . . .'

'You and he getting married?' Kendra put in for her quickly and uttered a slightly self-mocking half laugh. 'No, I just figured it was time I had a change of scene, that's all. It definitely has nothing to do with you and

Darby, I can assure you.' With a hopefully comforting smile.

The corners of Vivian's mouth curved softly upwards in thankful acknowledgment, although her clear blue eyes still continued their thoughtful regard. 'Something is upsetting you, though, isn't it, Kendra? Or someone,' she surmised slowly. 'It's not Mike you're leaving town to escape, is it?'

'No, of course not!' was the nervously rushed refutation. 'Why would I leave town to escape him? Or—or anyone else, for that matter. I told you, I just feel like a change, that's all.'

'So unexpectedly? And so ... unpredictably?' Vivian countered, sceptically wry. 'You've certainly never expressed any desire to leave Goldfield before.'

Kendra hunched a painstakingly dismissive shoulder. 'So now I've changed my mind. Not that I know why you should think something's upsetting me, anyway.'

'Mainly, I expect, as a result of Darby saying you've been acting quite out of character of late, but now even I can see that you've changed in some imperceptible way. There's almost an air of—of ...' she seemed to be struggling for the right word and Kendra gulped in an apprehensive breath as she waited, '... flatness, of pensiveness about you, that I've never seen previously. You're usually very much more animated and self-assured. And if it isn't Mike who's the cause of it, then since the only other thing that's different in town these days is the added presence of Rogan Faulkner, I can only presume he's the one to have brought about such a marked change in you.' Tilting her head, she surveyed the younger girl in watchful enquiry.

An abrupt hotness flooded Kendra's face and for a moment she couldn't speak due to the strangling lump that had leapt into her throat. 'Th-that's ridiculous!' she just managed to get out at last. 'You know how— how I feel about gold miners and prospectors. I've said it often enough, even where Darby's concerned. I wouldn't want one as—as a gift!'

'Except for one particular one who not only happens to be extremely likeable, but who's also managed to get under your skin more than you wanted, or expected him to, hmm?' She continued before Kendra could even define, let alone voice a suitable reply. 'As I'm surprised Darby didn't realise, too. But then, men rarely do seem to be as perceptive in such matters as we women, do they?' Smiling ruefully, Vivian obviously took an acceptance of her assumption to be a foregone conclusion.

In the meantime, Kendra cast about frantically for some plausible disclaimer, starting to panic when nothing immediately presented itself, and then almost collapsing in Mike's arms with gratitude when he chose that moment to claim her for a dance.

'If you'll excuse us . . .' She smiled weakly at Vivian as Mike began leading her into the middle of the floor.

'Him—probably. You—I'll have to think about,' came the humorously eloquent reply.

'What was that supposed to mean?' quizzed Mike as they joined the other couples to form a circle for Frank Edgar's nominated Picnic Polka.

'Oh, nothing of any importance,' relief enabled Kendra to discount airily. 'Just the result of my leaving our conversation, I expect.'

He nodded, losing interest, and presently there was no opportunity for anything but bare snatches of speech as the music began again and they sprang into the fast moving heel-toe steps of the polka.

Like a lot of the dances it was one where partners were continually changed, and as she swung from one

to another Kendra could feel herself gradually starting
to relax for the first time that evening and enjoy as
usual the happy, laughter-filled atmosphere.

Then all at once, as she swung away from her most
recent partner, she found it was Rogan she was
automatically linking arms with, his good-looking face
she was smiling into, and with a dismayed swallow she
immediately dropped her gaze to the vicinity of his
broad chest, her smile abruptly disappearing.

'I'm sorry, if I'd realised I would have joined a
different group,' she declared stiffly, indicating the
other two circles of skipping forms.

'Oh, don't be so idiotic!' he rebuked as he clasped
her in the waltz hold and propelled her into their
forward steps.

'Well, you were the one who instructed me to stay
out of your way!' she retorted defensively as they
turned and began moving back again.

Releasing, they faced each other, clapping their
right hands together three times. 'I was hardly likely
to mean under these circumstances, however, was I?'
he returned mockingly.

Clapping their left hands together now, Kendra
raised an implicit brow. 'Just another instance of your
not liking to be too precise, hmm?' she sniped.

Rogan muttered something under his breath that
she couldn't quite catch, but when they went on to
clap both hands together hers felt a decided sting on
connecting with his and she bit at her lip despairingly,
wishing once more that she could have stayed at home.
Then just as swiftly as they had come together, they
were shortly swinging apart again without another
word being spoken.

Glad when the dance was finished, Kendra refused
all offers for the next one, preferring to sit talking to
Maureen Fisher instead, whose now advanced stage of

pregnancy precluded her from joining in such active proceedings. Her husband, Jon, forbearingly made up the numbers in a set for Strip the Willow by dancing with the eight-year-old daughter of one of the local station managers.

'Well, thanks to Darby's new friend, the town's interest in mining has certainly been resurrected this week, hasn't it?' remarked Maureen cheerfully. 'And will continue that way, too, I guess, since I hear it's more or less definite now that the area's to be mined again.' Her brown eyes viewed the girl seated next to her interestedly. 'Have you any idea when construction's likely to begin?'

'Not for some months, I suppose.' Kendra shrugged indifferently. 'You know how it is, even after the applications are lodged they still have to be vetted by the Mines Department in Brisbane, plus a Government survey of the area conducted, of course. Then they're advertised in the newspapers, heard in the Warden's Court, and only after all that's been done does the Minister finally get around to actually granting the leases. It's a long process.' She shrugged again.

'The more so now they're testing Darby's lease as well, I expect, as I can't see them submitting any applications until they're finished there, so if they do decide to include it they can all be lodged together,' Maureen mused. She paused, giving her head a light shake and laughing. 'And what a surprise that eventuality gave everyone! Just the thought of Darby, of all people, being willing to transfer his claim was simply incredible. No one ever believed such a day would come.'

'No, well, I gather he felt it was just too good an opportunity to miss,' Kendra relayed shortly, wishing her friend would drop the subject.

Unaware, Maureen continued enthusiastically.

'With many more opportunities to come for the town as a whole, hopefully, once the project does actually get under way, what with the best employment prospects Goldfield's had in decades, increased trade, accommodation required for construction crews, and so on. Oh, yes, I can imagine we'll see quite a few changes in this town, thanks to the Faulkners.'

'Mmm, changes at least some of us would rather do without,' put in Kendra in dampening tones.

'Oh, Kendra, I can't believe you really mean that!' her friend half laughed, half frowned. 'Besides, no one else I've spoken to seems to feel like that. They all reckon they're looking forward to added prosperity. For myself, I'm just hoping that it might mean we could perhaps support our own hospital here in town in future, even if only a very small one, so we wouldn't have to travel all the way to Red Gap for medical treatment. Which in my present condition is quite a chore, I can tell you, especially having to endure that bumpy road every time a check-up is required. As it is, when I go over there for my next one on Wednesday the doctor's already recommended that I stay there for the following couple of weeks until the baby's born, whereas I'd much rather be in familiar surroundings at such a time.'

'I can see your point,' conceded Kendra sympathetically, never having viewed their relative isolation from such a position before. 'Although Jon will be staying there with you as well, won't he?'

'Only for the last week,' sighed Maureen regretfully. 'Unfortunately, we can't really afford for us both to be there any longer than that.'

Then maybe if Jon had applied for a job on one of the surrounding properties instead of fooling around with his damned mine all the time they could have afforded it! gibed Kendra to herself, but refrained from saying anything of the kind aloud, knowing it would only hurt her friend. In place of it she tried her best to be encouraging.

'Oh, well, maybe you could comfort yourself with the thought that next time there just might be a hospital here in Goldfield, as you hope. I suppose it is a possibility if there's an influx of people associated with the mine into the town.'

'I'll be keeping my fingers crossed, that's for sure!' advised Maureen ruefully. 'Because both Jon and I like kids and we certainly plan to have more than one.'

'Can you afford them?' the drily expressive retort was out this time before Kendra could think to stall it.

'We'll manage,' Maureen asserted, giving her a wry look. 'Although it would be less of a strain, naturally, if Jon could get work at the mine when it opens. He's been saying he wouldn't mind giving it a try.'

'You mean, like Darby, he's actually considering relinquishing his own claim?' Kendra stared at her in amazement. Hers certainly wasn't the only life the Faulkners' arrival in town had had a profound effect upon, apparently!

'Well, not exactly giving it up altogether. More like just continuing with it as a hobby when time permits,' clarified Maureen. Followed by a whimsically grinned, 'I suspect it's the idea of still being involved in mining that's made it acceptable, as it probably did for Darby as well.'

It wasn't a thought that had occurred to Kendra previously, but on reflection she was inclined to think Maureen could be right. Nevertheless, where Jon was concerned, she did still feel obliged to voice a note of caution. 'Provided, that is, that they do intend employing people from Goldfield and not just bringing in others from elsewhere who are already on their payroll.'

Maureen hunched a philosophical shoulder and nodded towards the middle of the floor where the dancers' formations had started to break up now that the dance had concluded. 'We'll soon know about that, then, because unless I'm very much mistaken that's precisely what Jonno will be discussing with Rogan Faulkner right at this moment.'

Glancing involuntarily at the two men, Kendra found her gaze waywardly concentrating on the taller of them, drinking in his muscular form, his strong-boned features, his firm sensuous mouth that even now was curving into a wide smile that promptly devastated her emotions.

Oh, God, how she wished she could turn back the clock, withdraw everything that had been said, make a new beginning. She loved him to distraction, and nothing would have made her more delirious with happiness than to have been able to spend the rest of her life with him, but with a feeling of utter desolation she knew it was merely an impossible dream. She could only sit staring at him, spellbound, wanting, and totally oblivious to her surroundings.

'Hey! Did you hear what Jon just said?'

Maureen's excited voice abruptly snapped Kendra out of her anguished reverie, only to discover herself being scrutinised quizzically by Rogan in return now that he was alone, and crimsoning with mortification she hurriedly turned her attention to her companions.

'I—I'm sorry. Wh-what did you say?' she faltered.

'I said . . . Did you hear what Jon just said?' repeated Maureen. And mirthfully to her husband, 'I think she must have been daydreaming. Although how anybody could with the noise in here, I don't know.'

'No, I'm sorry, I didn't hear,' Kendra replied jerkily, resisting the urge to see if Rogan's gaze was still focused in their direction. 'What did you say, Jon?'

Despite her husband having been the one asked, it was Maureen who answered, with zest. 'That Rogan says they will be hiring people from Goldfield, and that they'll definitely keep Jon in mind when they start employing! Isn't that great?'

'Yes, very. I'm pleased for you, Jon.' Kendra smiled across at the young man, genuinely pleased on his behalf.

'Ah, there you are! I've been looking everywhere for you.' It was Curry's voice that claimed Kendra's attention this time as he came to a stop in front of her. 'I've been told the next dance is to be a Pride of Erin—which is a little more my speed compared to those jigs and reels,' with wryly twitching lips, 'and I would deem it a pleasure if you would consent to be my partner.' He smiled down at her.

Surmising it would be considered strange if she didn't dance with at least one of the Faulkners—not that she had anything against Curry, anyway, and there was the added advantage that one remained with the same partner throughout on this particular occasion—Kendra rose to her feet with her own lips lifting at the corners in response.

'Thank you, kind sir.' She bobbed her head demurely as she accepted his extended arm.

As it happened, it turned out to be the most enjoyable period of Kendra's evening until then, for as Curry obviously knew the steps as well as she did, there was no need for either of them to concentrate on anything but their thankfully inconsequential conversation and the amusing anecdotes he kept her entertained with, which succeeded in putting some of the sparkle back into her eyes and even had her dissolving into helpless giggles at one stage.

'Can we share the joke, too?' came the overly sweet and coyly made query from Genevieve as she and

Rogan—who else? grimaced Kendra acidly—moved in beside them just as she was beginning to recover some of her composure following the episode.

'Oh, Rogan already knows the story, and I doubt it would appeal to you, Genevieve, concerning as it does the less—er—glamorous side of gold mining,' Curry replied negligently.

'Then I'm surprised it did to Kendra either knowing her views on the subject!' The redhead's evidently nettled return came close to being snapped.

Curry's eyes crinkled in his weathered, suntanned face. 'Which just goes to show, doesn't it?' He smiled somewhat enigmatically as their steps started parting them again.

'What did he mean by that?' Kendra just heard Genevieve puzzle to Rogan before they moved out of earshot, but although she wasn't certain of the meaning herself she was glad she couldn't hear Rogan's reply. His expression during the brief interplay had been as quelling as she had ever seen it.

And more than likely due, or at least in part, to his father having declined to regale Genevieve with the story that had so amused herself, Kendra mused gloomily. She'd noticed that the other girl had been his most favoured partner so far, even though Genevieve was obligingly—or shrewdly—giving her attention to Rex during the breaks between dances. The fact that he was a member of the band, and therefore conveniently otherwise engaged for the majority of the time, allowing her to continue playing the coquette with both men.

Around ten-thirty the band called a well-deserved halt while supper was served. Long trestle tables in the kitchen were covered with gaily patterned cloths, the plates piled high with food distributed thereon. There were assorted sandwiches and sausage rolls, cheesecakes and cream-decorated tarts, chocolate-coated and coconut-dusted lamingtons, six-inch high fairy light sponges filled with jam and cream, meringues and pavlovas, jelly cakes, fruit cakes, cream puffs and chocolate-covered nut slices. At a separate table the big teapots were filled, the jugs of milk and bowls of sugar being placed at intervals along the table bearing the food so no hold-ups would occur as everyone helped themselves to tea or coffee at the smaller table.

Soon everybody had a plate of their own bearing a selection of tasty morsels in one hand and a cup of hot liquid in the other, some wandering back to the seats in the hall before consuming theirs, others making use of the steps leading into the building, but many more choosing the grass outside where it was decidedly cooler.

Intending to join the ranks of the latter, Kendra headed down the steps and seeing Maureen and Jon, together with Mike, already seated some distance away, prepared to join them.

It was a beautifully clear night, the sky above star-filled, the yellow orb of the moon providing a dusky luminance where the lights from the hall didn't reach, the only sounds apart from muted chatter and laughter those of the nightly insects and the occasional distinctive call of a hunting boobook owl.

With her attention fixed on where she was going, it wasn't until a voice sounded beside her that Kendra realised someone had joined her.

'You know, you really should be more careful,' cautioned Genevieve with a faint hint of mockery in her tone.

Thinking she must have been implying she had dropped something, Kendra stopped, looking about her first and then down at her plate. 'There doesn't appear to be . . .'

'Oh, I wasn't referring to that,' the other girl cut her off with a dismissive half laugh. 'I was meaning . . . with regard to Rogan.'

Kendra inhaled deeply, warily. 'In what way?'

'Mainly, I suppose, by looking at him as you were doing earlier,' Genevieve revealed with something of a sardonic smirk. 'To say you were wearing your heart on your sleeve at the time would be an absolute understatement, believe me. One would have to have been blind not to notice. And it's such a pity.' She shook her head in doubtful sorrow.

'Because you've ambitions in that direction yourself?' quipped Kendra in defence, despite the shuddering sense of despair that was assailing her. Oh, God, had she really been *that* obvious? Had anyone else seen? *Had Rogan?* After all, she recalled his return survey *had* been quite intent. Unable to bear to contemplate it further, she gave a falsely nonchalant toss of her head and pushed out a careless laugh. 'In any case, it sounds to me as if you need your eyes tested, Genevieve. I mean to say, with my record, would I *really* be likely to fall for someone in the mining game?'

Genevieve merely smiled complacently. 'If the man in question was attractive enough, and . . . felt like proving, for his own satisfaction, that he could overcome your dislike, why not? Because we do know they all seem quite unable to resist such a challenge, don't they?' She paused, her mouth shaping with self-satisfaction. 'While as for my having ambitions in that direction . . . well, I'm certainly flattered by your acknowledgment that it's *my* choice as to whether it's Rogan or Rex that I marry, but as it so happens I've already decided—even if Rogan is proving most reluctant to accept my verdict, poor pet.' She uttered an exaggerated sigh of compassion.

The revelation temporarily put all other thoughts out of Kendra's mind. 'You're saying, you're going to marry Rex, after all?' she gasped incredulously. The way Genevieve had been behaving, and now with Rogan's wealth as an extra incentive, she had quite expected the younger man to have been sweetly, but decisively discarded.

'Of course,' Genevieve confirmed with a trill of laughter. 'Oh, I admit I was considering Rogan for a while, but then I got to thinking how much longer I've known Rex, how much he loves me. It made me realise how much I loved him, too, and that I'd really only been having a last fling with Rogan, as it were.' She shrugged deprecatingly. 'So you see, it *was* purely on your behalf that I warned you about making your feelings for Rogan so evident. Knowing how he feels about you, I just didn't want you to be hurt even more, that's all. We Goldfielders should stick together, when all's said and done, shouldn't we?'

Not believing for a moment that loyalty of any kind had prompted the other girl's remarks, even though she couldn't exactly now put her finger on any other reason, Kendra still prudently decided to keep her own counsel where her feelings were concerned, but at the same time couldn't refrain from enquiring in as wryly amused a tone as she could manage, 'Oh, and just how *does* Rogan feel about me?' Then promptly wondered if she had some weird liking for pain that she should even have asked.

'I—well—I'd really rather not say,' Genevieve parried uncomfortably.

Or was it a pretended discomfort? pondered Kendra cynically. Whichever, and faked or not, it only served to endorse her earlier surmise that whatever Genevieve had to say wouldn't be pleasant, and so she availed herself of the opportunity—inwardly grateful, outwardly indifferent—the hesitation had presented to leave the matter well alone.

'Okay. I wasn't all that interested, anyhow.' She shrugged, starting to move forward again.

'Oh, but . . .' Genevieve began and then halted abruptly on apparently remembering she was supposed to be exhibiting reluctance. Recovering, she assumed an understanding demeanour. 'No, I don't blame you for changing your mind. I expect I would, too, if I was in your place. It must be horribly distressing to be infatuated with someone who so obviously wants nothing to do with you.'

And especially when there's someone like you to so thoughtfully rub it in! gibed Kendra brokenly to herself, her fingers clenching about the cup in her hand. With a supreme effort she permitted no such despondency to show on her features, however, when she slanted the older girl a taunting look over her shoulder.

'Yes, I should think it definitely would be,' she agreed flippantly. 'Fortunately, though, I'm nothing of the kind.' Shaking her head, she gave a lightly amused laugh. 'You always did have an overly fertile imagination, Genevieve. As you really should know, *all* prospectors, attractive or otherwise, have always been anathema to me. So whatever emotion you apparently *think* you saw in my expression at some time, I really do suggest you try and come up with something more credible than the one you did, because that's so improbable as to be ludicrous.' And with a pitying smile of her own she resumed walking.

This time Genevieve let her go without comment, merely staring after her for a time with a somewhat less certain, but plainly out of humour, look on her face before whirling rapidly and stalking back to the hall.

'So what were you and our publican's gem of a daughter discussing with such dedication?' asked Maureen wryly as Kendra finally joined her friends.

'Oh, nothing much,' she disclaimed with studied breeziness. 'I think she was just feeling the need to blow her own trumpet, as usual, by informing me she has both Rex and Rogan jumping to her tune.' Omitting anything of a more personal nature.

'And it took her that long?' Maureen grinned, brows lifting. 'She must be slipping.'

'No, well, for some unknown reason she also went to great lengths to let me know that she'd made her choice between the two of them, apparently, and that Rex is to be the lucky man, after all.'

'I would've said that made Faulkner the lucky one,' put in Jon drily, and bringing wry endorsing smiles to all their faces. 'She'll lead whoever she marries a merry dance, I reckon.'

'That's for sure!' echoed Mike in pungent accents before going on to talk about something else.

Once supper was finished, the many hands available in the kitchen made light work of the washing up and clearing away, and then most of the children who were still awake went to join their younger brothers and sisters who had already retired to the room at the back of the hall where makeshift beds allowed them to sleep comfortably until it was time to go home.

The members of the band were picking up their instruments again—Frank Edgar hastily concluding the re-lubrication of his dry throat with the last of the beer in a can provided from the stock of such beverages the men usually kept in the back of their vehicles on such occasions—when Kendra re-entered the hall and immediately had her wrist encircled by strong fingers.

'This dance is mine, I believe,' stated Rogan arbitrarily and started towing her towards a set that was being formed.

'No! I . . .' Kendra halted, her face becoming tinged with self-conscious colour on realising her protest had been loud enough to draw surprised, and unwanted, attention to them.

Knowing her predicament, Rogan eyed her mockingly. 'You don't have a choice, unless you *do* wish to create a scene, of course.'

'Then why commandeer me,' it certainly hadn't been a request! 'for a dance at all?' she demanded, her heart thudding heavily against her ribs.

'Because I figured it would generate even more speculation if I didn't since it was your and Darby's house I stayed in for most of my time here.'

Of course! Why else? It surely wouldn't have been because he *wanted* to dance with her. 'I see,' she murmured flatly.

'Ladies and gentlemen, take your partners please for the Queensland Backstep,' sang out Frank from the stage at the end of the hall, and had Kendra chew at her lip in dismay as Rogan led them into the longways set.

Why did it have to be this particular dance? she despaired. Although it wasn't one where partners were in particularly close contact, it was still one where they remained constant. Worse still, in one section it called for kisses to be exchanged, and not only once but ten times in all due to there being that number of couples in each set! Normally, they were occurrences that were treated light-heartedly, a peck on the cheek more often than not despite some of the younger ones sometimes choosing to execute the move with a little more ardour, but this evening Kendra could only anticipate it with consternation. Feeling as she did, she couldn't be certain she wouldn't somehow betray herself in such an unnerving situation.

As they formed their lines facing one another, women on one side and men on the other, Kendra grasped momentarily at the hope that Rogan wouldn't know the dance and therefore might miss the move, but as the music began and she noted the sureness of his steps as the two lines moved inward preparing to bow—abruptly reminding her that there had been another such reel before supper—she had to reject it as wishful thinking.

Now, she realised suddenly, the lines were converging again, to kiss this time instead of bowing, but with her hands linked with those of the girls on each side of her ready to make arches for the men to pass under, Kendra was helpless to do anything but submit when the cheek she determinedly presented to Rogan was ignored and a hand cupping the back of her head ensured that it was her lips that connected with his. That the pressure was only fleeting was no consolation to her whatsoever, because on their facing each other again she could see a trace of the old, lazy teasing was back in his eyes and her pulse raced in panic at the thought of what may have precipitated its return. He hadn't been able to see through her frantic efforts to appear unmoved, had he?

For Kendra the dance progressed all too slowly, and yet simultaneously all too rapidly did those times when Rogan kissed her seem to approach. And each time they did her agitation grew ungovernably, so that on the last occasion her mouth literally trembled beneath his when he claimed it for slightly longer and with decidedly more thoroughness.

It was all she could do to remain until the dance finished—she had never felt quite so miserable, or so churned up in her life!—and almost before the last note had been played she was breaking away and heading out of the building in the hope that some solitude would help calm her troubled thoughts and emotions, and thus restore to her at least some semblance of poise.

CHAPTER SEVEN

THANKFUL to discover she was the only one outside, Kendra made her way around to the back of the hall, knowing few people ever bothered going that far when they left the building for a breath of fresh air. Stepping past a rampant bougainvillaea that had been allowed to run wild, she rested her folded arms on the top rail of a rickety, old wooden fence that had originally enclosed the whole grounds completely but now only survived in sections, and stared unseeingly at the mine-crated landscape beyond.

She was of half a mind to leave altogether and go home, but aware that would only create talk and quite likely even a puzzled search if she did so without advising anyone, she reluctantly decided against it. She really didn't feel up to parrying any more questions that evening. All she wanted was to ensure she didn't give rise to any further speculation of the dismaying kind Genevieve had confronted her with, or a possible repeat of that last disastrous dance with Rogan. Just the memory of her lack of control was enough to have her flushing hotly again and castigating herself angrily for having permitted her emotions to get so far out of hand. Prior to Rogan's arrival in town, she had always been secure in the knowledge that it was very much her head that was in charge.

How long she remained there immersed in her own thoughts, Kendra wasn't sure, although from the brief penetration of her consciousness by the different tunes the band had been playing she supposed it must have been some time, but the unexpected sound of rustling grass as someone else also ventured beyond the mown area suddenly interrupted her musings and had her stiffening defensively as she turned to see who it might be.

'So this is where you've been hiding.' Rogan's wryly drawling voice reached out to her as he, too, stepped past the unruly bougainvillaea.

Kendra watched his approach with wide and wary eyes that were shimmering pools of almost navy blue in the shadowed light. 'I don't know why you'd think that,' she disputed in as disdainful a tone as she could manifest. 'I merely didn't feel like dancing, that's all.'

'And you always hide out here when you don't feel like dancing, hmm?'

His refusal to accept her explanation perturbed. As did the supicion that he may have been finding the situation amusing. There wasn't sufficient light to tell from his expression.

'Yes, as a matter of fact I do,' she lied on a stilted note. In truth, she had never before *not* wanted to participate in any of the bush dances. 'But certainly not to hide. Just for the peace and quiet.' Hoping he might take the hint and depart.

He didn't, but took a further step that brought him to the fence beside her instead, leaning back against a post with his arms folded across his muscular chest, his thickly lashed eyes surveying her leisurely from the top of her stiffly erect head to her somewhat restively moving feet.

'Which you evidently felt in need of so badly that you could hardly wait for our dance to finish before rushing off in search of it.' Drily.

Positive he was making fun of her now, Kendra angled her chin a fraction higher. 'It was hot, and as it also happens to be much cooler out here . . .' She shrugged defiantly. 'Not that I can see what concern it is of yours, in any event.' Pausing, her tone became infused with a protectively mocking nuance. 'Or even why you should have apparently come looking for me at all, if it comes to that. We've had our obligatory dance, so why not simply leave it at that ... and be grateful that I've considerately removed myself from your presence as you previously, and so succinctly, instructed I should.'

'And as I'm beginning to realise I should have been.' Rogan's own voice began revealing traces of sardonic emphasis now. 'However, obligation seemed to dictate once again that I at least say goodbye before Curry and I presently take our leave.'

'You're not staying until the end?' Surprise shocked Kendra into questioning.

'Since we understand it's likely to continue for a couple more hours yet, and as we want to be away by five in the morning, no, we've decided to call it a night,' he advised dispassionately.

'Oh!' she said lamely, biting at her lip, and abruptly struck by the aching realisation that this would quite possibly be the last time she ever saw him. Now that the moment had actually arrived, she found herself capriciously wanting to delay it for as long as possible. 'Well, I wish you both a safe journey, of course, and—and ...' She halted as her voice started to thicken traitorously, and swallowing hard, tried again. 'You'll be returning to your mine in the Gulf, will you?'

'Curry will be, but I'll be heading back into the Territory, to our headquarters in Alice. That's where all the paperwork required to get this new undertaking on the go will be finalised.'

'And have you any idea when you're likely to know if—if Darby is to be included in the enterprise?' She ventured to sound out.

Rogan didn't immediately say, but remarked in lieu, and in a return to less impassive tones, 'Mmm, he told me he'd already informed you about that. Naturally there's no need to ask just what your reaction was on hearing of it, is there?' A crooking brow lent his features a satiric cast. 'So what scheming plan did you promptly envisage I had in mind this time?'

Kendra supposed she deserved that and dropped her gaze self-consciously. 'None, actually, when Darby explained it was his idea,' she murmured, not a little surprised that her brother apparently hadn't seen fit to tell him the whole story.

A hand beneath her chin unexpectedly tilted her face up to his. 'But plenty before that came to light, hmm?' he deduced astutely, caustically.

She ran the tip of her tongue over dry lips. 'I— well . . .'

'Precisely!' There was a derisive bite in the word as he removed his hand in an equally spurning gesture. 'And now you suddenly want to know when, and if, his lease is to be included, do you? Well, I'm afraid you're simply going to have to wait, the same as everyone else, for the answer to that one, sweetheart! Or were you hoping for some earlier, inside information so you can make your exit from town that much sooner? Is that what's at the back of it? Because you just can't take the idea of not being Darby's keeper any more?'

'No!' she gasped, appalled. 'Nor have I ever seen myself as his keeper either! It's only *you* who ever thought that!'

'With good reason, perhaps?' he countered mockingly, and had her eyes flashing stormily in response. 'Because if that isn't the reason for your sudden desire to—er—spread your wings, then what is? Your inability to accept the thought of someone else aking over your position once Darby and Vivian do marry?'

'No!' Although categorical, her denial none the less carried a note of anguish caused by the realisation that he evidently couldn't have thought any less of her if he'd tried. The knowledge tore at her emotions and had her shoulders drooping. Without looking at him, she continued in a small throaty voice, 'But since my reasons for leaving are no business of yours, in any case, I think this is an appropriate time for us to part, so if you don't mind I'll just say goodbye and relieve you of the necessity to remain in my company any longer.' She valiantly extended a slim-fingered, and slightly unsteady, hand towards him.

Acknowledging the gesture, Rogan enclosed her trembling fingers within the hard strength of his, but didn't immediately release them again as his glance settled on her downcast features. 'You're shaking,' he observed with an oblique twist to his shapely mouth. 'In temper . . . or trepidation?'

'Neither,' she disclaimed in sombre tones, vainly attempting to withdraw her hand from his.

'And if I disagree that this is an appropriate time to part?'

Kendra's eyes flickered up to his momentarily in confusion. 'There's no reason for you to want to prolong it.' She hesitated, her spirits sinking even further. 'Unless, of course, there are more uncomplimentary remarks you wish to make before you go.'

'Yours always having been laudatory in the extreme, I suppose?' Rogan half laughed sardonically.

She chewed at the inside of her lip in regret, hazarding sadly, 'For which you want to extract full revenge before taking your departure, is that it?'

'No, that isn't . . .!' he began on a suddenly

roughening note, then halted, freeing her at last, and dragged a hand through his hair. Abruptly his gaze narrowed, his eyes darkening dangerously, and sending a shiver of latent wariness speeding down her spine. 'Although maybe I should, at that! It's obviously about time someone damn well taught you what a fine line you tread at times!' Jerking her against him, his lips swiftly captured hers with a compelling, searing dominance that brooked no resistance.

Kendra uttered a faint, smothered sound in the back of her throat, struggling desperately to regain her freedom, but to no avail. There was no escape from either the iron-hard bands of his encircling arms or the burning demands of his mouth. Instead, there was only the despairing knowledge that he had not only snatched from her the ability to resist, but was gradually, insistently wresting from her the will to as well.

Dazed, shaken by the pervasive warmth beginning to flood through her, she felt as if her blood was on fire, her bones melting, and with a soft moan her lips opened tremulously to his, her body moulding itself pliantly to his ruggedly muscular shape. In turn, Rogan's kisses became more leisurely, inviting rather than exacting now, his hands trailing caressingly down her back to her hips, stirring an even more fiery arousal.

Of their own accord, Kendra's arms coiled tightly about his neck, her fingers entwining within his thick, black hair, surrendering herself to both him and sensations never before experienced. She loved him with every fibre of her being. Loved the clean masculine smell of him, the sense of power and strength that was such an innate part of him, the unbelievable stimulation of his touch, the drugging quality of his kisses that evoked such ungovernable longings within her. The awareness that she would never again know the pleasure of being held so in his arms only served to heighten her emotions to an almost desperate degree.

Along with such consciousness, however, slowly came the recollection of her conversation with Genevieve, and as everything that had been said suddenly flooded back into her mind—including that girl's disclosure that Rogan had been loath to accept her decision to marry Rex—Kendra gave a gasp and had twisted out of Rogan's arms before he realised what she was about.

'No!' she protested hoarsely, shaking her head, her breath coming in short painful gulps as she continued backing away. 'You're not using me to alleviate your disappointment!'

'Damn you, Kendra!' Rogan gritted savagely, his eyes glinting greenly, his chest rising and falling as rapidly as her own as he made a grab for her which she just managed to elude. 'What the hell are you on about now?'

'As if you don't know!' she scorned, trying furiously to disregard the ache in her heart that was almost too much to be borne. 'But you've had your revenge now—which undoubtedly must be very gratifying f-for you,' she caught back the sob that rose in her throat, 'so why don't you just take yourself back to where you came from and let me live in the hope that I never set eyes on you again!' A choking cry did escape her now as she spun about and began running with stumbling steps for the safety offered by the numbers in the hall.

'That suits me just fine!' His endorsement lashed out harshly after her. 'A respite from your bloody-minded contrariness will be no hardship whatsoever!'

'Likewise, your deceitful, false-hearted, and unwelcome self!' she half turned to hurl back in scathing accents, and then fled even faster on seeing him take a step forward, his expression tight-lipped and threatening in its grimness.

Struggling to appear her normal self, if a little wanly, Kendra only remained at the hall for as long as it took to add her farewell to those already being proferred to Curry, and only that when Rogan was engaged elsewhere. Then pleading tiredness to Darby and Vivian, as well as her friends, she declined Mike's offer to walk her home with the contention that there was no call for him to curtail his enjoyment or his evening simply because she didn't feel like staying any longer, she made her way back to the house rapidly. Her troubled thoughts being an odd mixture of relief at not having to pretend any more that everything was as usual, and an agonising desolation at knowing it wasn't, and what was more, probably never would be again.

A month or so later Darby was to sigh heavily on observing his sister emerging from the master bedroom with a suitcase in her hand. 'You're starting to pack already?'

'I thought I may as well.' Kendra shrugged. 'I'm taking a fair amount with me.' Her lips shaped into a wry smile. 'I'm not planning on leaving earlier than I said, though, if that's what you're thinking. I promised to stay here and look after things, including Jimmy of course, until you and Vivian returned from your honeymoon, and I will.' He and Vivian had finally set a date for their marriage which was now only three days away. 'So there's no need for you to look so worried about it.'

He shook his head. 'That's not what worries me . . . as you should know. It's the feeling I've still got that it's us forcing you out.'

'Which couldn't be further from the truth, as *I've* tried to convince you before.' She gave a short little laugh. 'Honestly, Darby, I simply decided I'd like a change, nothing more. I'm certainly not going off in a huff because of losing my position, or whatever, in the house,' as someone else had once accused, 'I can assure you.'

A brief look of relief registered on Darby's face before it assumed a thoughtful cast again. 'Vivian's wondered a couple of times ... if it could have something to do with Rogan,' he abruptly divulged, his glance becoming more intent.

Perish her prospective sister-in-law's perception! grimaced Kendra. It was something of a strain for her to reply in a supposedly amused voice, but she thought she carried it off reasonably well. 'How could it possibly?' she countered. 'I've never been so positively serene as I have since he left.'

'Nor so quiet, spiritless, introspective, not to say lacklustre.'

'I—I've had a lot of things on my mind,' she hedged nervously. 'What with your marriage approaching and all that entails, my going away, and—and everything.'

Darby continued eyeing her watchfully for a few moments, but when her blue eyes remained resolutely challenging his, he lifted a broad shoulder and allowed with a fond smile, 'Okay, love, if that's the way you want it.'

On the verge of taking him to task for his suspect wording, Kendra then thought better of it. Knowing just how frail her defences really were on the subject she judged it wisest not to pursue it. 'Yes, well ...' she merely murmured obscurely, and changed the topic completely. 'So where are you off to this morning? The mine again?' Although not having worked it since the geologists had done their tests there, he had been doing a lot of sorting and clearing of the many bits and pieces that had accumulated at the site over the years.

'For the last time, I hope.' He nodded. 'If not beforehand, then I should have word from Rogan and Curry at least by the time Vivian and I return as to what's going to happen out there.'

'You think no news really could be good news in this instance?' she hazarded diffidently, aware how anxiously he was awaiting that word regarding the Good Cheer's, and therefore his, prospects.

'I keep telling myself it is,' he owned, smiling ruefully. 'Especially when I remember what the geologists had to say when they sent those last samples off to be assayed. However . . .' He raised his shoulders graphically. 'Even if there is payable ore there, and good reserves of it, that's still no guarantee Rogan and Curry will come to the aid of the party, so to speak. I mean, I saw the opportunity and took a long shot in even putting the proposal to them, but they could still decide against it. There's only ever been the two of them included in their activities to date.'

Kendra put her arm about his waist, returning his smile encouragingly. 'Then I suppose we'll just have to keep our fingers crossed for you a little longer, won't we?'

'For you too, love,' he amended in determined tones. 'If anything does come of it, you're entitled to a share of whatever I receive. Probably more than I am, if it comes to that,' with a remorseful shaping of his lips. 'You're the one who's really carried us all these years.'

'I've no complaints,' she dismissed her efforts casually. 'Well, I only did have because I didn't want you to spend your whole life down that hole, or for you to be in danger,' honesty made her add wryly.

'I know, little one.' He ruffled her hair affectionately.

Depositing the case she had been carrying beside her bedroom door, Kendra walked out to the kitchen with him, her thoughts turning inward. 'Did I too often give the impression of considering myself "my brother's keeper", Darby?' she asked pensively.

'Not to me you didn't, no.' He glanced down at her curiously. 'Why, did someone say you had?'

'Something of the sort,' she conceded as offhandedly as possible.

'Rogan?' Darby probed too astutely for her liking. He was becoming as disconcertingly shrewd as Vivian!

She waved a hand in an indeterminate movement. 'It could have been. I don't really remember,' she prevaricated.

'Well, if it was . . .' he chucked her under the chin in emphasis, 'it was only because he felt you shouldn't take life so seriously. And as much as it might surprise you, I heard him go in to bat for you quite a few times while he was here.'

'For me?' Kendra stared at him almost open-mouthed in astonishment. She found it hard to believe they were even talking about the same person. 'Against whom?'

'Genevieve.' Laconically dry. 'I gather she wasn't any too keen on him spending so much time in your company while he was working in the store, so whenever the chance presented itself she would acquaint him with what she apparently considered to be your shortcomings. Presumably, in the hope of coming out best from the comparison. Nevertheless, much to her chagrin Rogan would simply imply that whatever she said paled into insignificance by contending, "She's sure one hell of a bloody good little worker, though!" which, in view of Genevieve's as good as work*less* existence, not unnaturally, kind of took the wind out of her sails.'

'I see,' she murmured, grimacing to herself. A worker, was she? Just like some bullocks in a team were, and some weren't! she supposed. She should have known any unlikely defence of herself by Rogan Faulkner would only have been of such a qualified, impersonal kind! She pushed out a careless laugh. 'Oh well, I guess we can't all be lotus-eaters, can we?'

'Exactly!' Darby's voice took on a slightly exasperated note. 'He was complimenting you on *not* being one! Something Genevieve realised at least, even if you are too astoundingly stubborn to recognise . . . or admit the same!' He shook his head incredulously. 'Lord, but you're hard to understand sometimes of late, love.'

'I'm sorry,' she sighed, and then gave a covering, if shaky laugh. 'It would appear I might need that change of scene more than I originally thought.'

'It would seem you sure need something,' he averred. Pausing, he looked as if he was about to add something further, then he shrugged and opened the screen door, eyeing implicitly the strapless sunfrock she was wearing as he did so. 'You're not opening the store until later today?'

'No, I thought I might leave it for an hour or so. There's rarely much custom early on Wednesdays, and as I still have some finishing touches to put to the dress I'm wearing to the wedding I thought I'd do them this morning.'

'Okay, I'll see you some time later, then.' He stepped on to the verandah and prepared to let the door swing closed after him.

'And will that be before, or after, a visit to the pub?' Kendra enquired drily.

Darby grinned. 'Well . . . I do only have a few nights of bachelorhood left to me.'

'All right, all right, I get the message.' She waved him on his way, laughing. 'I'll expect you when I see you.'

With an even broader, confirming smile pulling at his lips, he lifted a finger to his temple in a carefree salute and descended the steps sprightly, while inside, Kendra's thoughts began turning to other matters.

Deciding to put on a load of washing before settling down to her sewing, she collected all the necessary articles to add to the pile already waiting in the laundry and then hurried down the steps with them. It only took her a short while to load the machine and set it going, but on stepping back out of the laundry she came to a sudden, benumbed halt on seeing Rogan's totally unexpected figure leaning idly against the post at the foot of the back steps.

Dressed exactly as she always pictured him, in hip-hugging jeans, drill shirt and dusty stock boots, his hat set at a sloping angle on his dark head, he looked so vital, so blatantly male, that she immediately felt an overwhelming ache inside. Time had apparently done nothing to diminish his power to tie her emotions in knots just at the sight of him, she realised in despair.

'Missed me?' he quizzed at length, a mocking slant catching at his firmly etched mouth.

Little did he know just how much! sighed Kendra, unable to take her eyes off him. But as it wasn't a question she considered it would be prudent to answer aloud, she merely waved a hand rather distractedly and stammered, 'D-Darby's not here. He—he just left for the m-mine.'

'I know. I've just spoken to him.'

The information had her eyes widening slightly, doubtfully. Why was he at the house, then? She began nibbling at her lower lip nervously, her hands unconsciously clenching and unclenching at her sides.

Apart from those few agitated gestures, however, his abrupt appearance appeared to have deprived her of the ability to move, for her feet felt as if they had taken root in the ground, her legs seeming to have become made of rubber.

'Well, as attractive a picture as you make, I still presume it's not your intention to stand there *all* day,' he drawled wryly when she still hadn't spoken again. 'So shall we go inside?' He levered himself away from the post lazily as if inviting her to precede him up the steps.

Still too stunned, flustered, and completely unsure of herself, Kendra only knew she wanted to avoid any closer contact with him. 'I—I have to open the store,' she all but croaked in mounting panic, her legs treacherously failing to respond to her efforts to move in the appropriate direction.

Rogan flexed a negligently dismissve shoulder. 'You're not dressed for working in there, and . . .' a smile slowly widened his mouth, warmly taunting, and utterly devastating in effect, 'Darby said you weren't planning on going across until later than usual this morning.'

With her pulse leaping erratically, she desperately attempted to counter it with a defiant lift of her head. 'So I changed my mind!'

'The minute you saw me, hmm?' He began pacing leisurely, but inexorably, towards her.

'No!' she refuted on a strangled note, her eyes rounding to deep pools of apprehension the nearer he came. 'Because I—I thought I heard someone arrive when I—I was in the laundry.' The invention was frantically voiced.

'They'll know where to find you,' Rogan asserted, drawing even closer, and making Kendra rue his knowledge regarding the store's operation.

'That isn't the point,' she tried to dispute, albeit a touch weakly.

'Then what is?'

Perhaps it was the fact that he was within perturbing feet of her now, but at last Kendra regained the use of her legs, and along with them a lessening of the stupefied state of her mind as she hastily took a few steps backward.

'The point is ... we have absolutely nothing to say to one another, so I just wish you'd go away and leave me alone! I don't know what brought you back to Goldfield so soon, but ...'

'But you were envisaging being gone before I arrived, huh?' he interposed, a goading light glinting in the depths of his eyes.

Kendra held her breath in dismay, but returned his gaze tenaciously. 'And why should I do that?'

'Now that comes under the heading of my second reason for being here,' he relayed, provokingly uninformative.

'The first being ...?' she queried hesitantly, not knowing quite what to expect but hoping it might prove distracting—to him at least!

'Since Curry and I had been invited to the wedding, anyway,' which had Kendra giving a startled, inward gasp, due to it being the first intimation she'd had of their possible attendance, 'I merely decided to come on ahead in order to give Darby a wedding present of sorts, but which I thought he may have preferred to have rather sooner than later,' Rogan disclosed in whimsical tones.

Could he possibly be meaning ...? 'You're saying, you've accepted his proposal concerning the Good Cheer?' She sought verification of her surmise part tentatively, part excitedly. The latter on her brother's behalf.

'Uh-huh!'

'Does he know yet?' Her burgeoning happiness for Darby was uncontrollable, bringing a bright sparkle to her eyes, a relieved curve to her lips, and for the moment monopolising her every thought.

Without removing his gaze from her suddenly animated features, Rogan nodded lazily. 'Mmm, I told him when I stopped to speak to him.'

'I'll bet he was pleased—to put it mildly,' she divined with the beginnings of a smile lifting the corners of her mouth.

'You could say that,' he understated wryly.

'And—and you're . . .' All at once she came to a rapid stop, as if abruptly remembering who she was talking to, her smile disappearing beneath discomfitedly compressing lips. Then out of the blue an avenue of escape came to mind and she was already preparing to move past him when she proposed, 'I must go and see Vivian, in case she doesn't know yet.'

'Oh, no, you don't, sweetheart!' Almost before she knew it, Rogan had hold of her arm and was pulling her back towards him. 'If Vivian doesn't know yet, which I strongly doubt, then Darby can tell her later. But *you're* staying right here! This time there isn't going to be any seeking refuge in crowded halls—or at Vivian's! It's just going to be you and me . . . and a showdown that's long overdue!'

'I don't know what you're talking about!' Kendra denied, trying wildly to break his hold. 'And—and if it's showdowns you're after, you've got the wrong girl, haven't you? I understood it was Genevieve's decision to marry Rex you were loath to accept!' Her eyes flashed jeeringly.

'*Loath to accept!*' Rogan stared at her momentarily in disbelief, and then broke into a deep-throated laugh that stirred her traitorous senses and sent her emotions

reeling. 'Are you kidding? *Relieved* to hear it, would
be more apt! My God, that girl clutches like a
Christmas beetle ... only she takes more convincing
before finally acknowledging she's not wanted!' He
paused, his expression taking a subtle turn. 'However,
I didn't come here to talk about Genevieve.'

'And I don't care why you came here! I just wish
you'd leave!' she blazed at him in sheer alarm as he
ignored her renewed attempts to break away and
began hauling her closer. 'What's more—let go of my
arm! How dare you think you can just walk in here
and treat me in any manner you choose!' Anger started
to come to her aid.

'Maybe I wouldn't have to if you weren't so bloody
capricious all the time!' he retorted roughly. 'But you
want me to release your arm? Okay, I will ... when we
get inside!' Without more ado he began dragging her
after him towards, and then up the steps. 'At least in
the house it should hopefully prove more difficult for
you to keep darting off in order to avoid the issue.'

'There is no issue, damn you!' she heaved, landing a
satisfactory thump in the middle of his broad back as
she stumbled up the steps behind him. Not that by so
much as a look did he even seem to be aware of the
blow. 'We're just poles apart, that's all! Or can't you
get that through your thick prospector's head?'

Pulling open the screen door, Rogan thrust her
inside before entering himself, immediately tossing his
hat on to the table. 'Ah, yes ... prospectors!' A
mocking smile crossed his mouth. 'That takes us right
back to where it all began, doesn't it, sweetheart?'

'Except that nothing did ever begin!' she contradicted protectively, wary of just what he was
implying.

'Didn't it? Even despite your obstinate adherence to
those stupid biases of yours?' A sharper note suddenly

entered his voice. 'Then how do *you* view what happens as a result of something like this?' He yanked her against him, his lips coming down on hers without warning, urgent, relentless, demanding responses she had to fight furiously against giving.

'No!' Kendra cried brokenly on managing to drag her mouth from his, and abruptly realising he wasn't holding her arm any more either, took to her heels and fled into the hallway.

At first she ran blindly, not knowing where to head for sanctuary, then on hearing Rogan so close behind her made for the sitting room where she knew the doors giving on to the verandah were open, hopefully providing freedom. Dodging his outstretched hand, she dived into the room and promptly tripped on a large sheepskin rug on the polished floor.

She could feel herself starting to fall backwards as her feet slid from under her, but although Rogan's reflexes were sharp enough to catch her as she went down, thereby managing to break her fall considerably, her momentum was still such that it eventually had them both toppling on to the fortunately cushioning floor covering. Kendra immediately made a scrambling effort to rise to her feet again, but Rogan had other ideas and by the simple expedient of pinning her beneath his long, muscular form ensured she remained exactly where she was.

Strong fingers trailed along the side of her jaw. 'You sure believe in literally leading a man a chase, don't you, Kendra?' he murmured in a voice as wry as his accompanying smile.

'Nobody asked you to—to come after me! In fact, as I recall, I requested j-just the opposite!' she panted, pummelling at his shoulders and trying to squirm free.

Rogan clamped her slender wrists to the sheepskin rug above her head with a determined hand. With the other he gently traced the outline of her soft mouth. 'While your lips said something else entirely,' he taunted indolently, his head lowering.

Kendra fought against him violently, straining to evade his descending mouth. His disturbing observations were too near the mark already! Finally, she was reduced to beseeching, 'Rogan, please . . . no!'

He shook his head slowly. 'Uh-uh, my precious, that's what you always say, but this time it's very definitely *yes*,' he declared on a deepening note, his mouth fastening over hers resolutely.

Immediately Kendra felt her heartbeat quicken even as she continued to fight him, her blood turning to liquid fire as the demanding pressure of his sensous mouth seared through her resistance. He was methodically, unsparingly, destroying her every defence, making her oblivious to everything but the feel and touch of him, arousing feelings, desires, she knew only he could ever satisfy, and to which, with a shuddering sigh, she at last surrendered. She loved him, wanted him, and if he guessed how she felt about him there just wasn't anything she could do about it. It was simply impossible to deny him, and her own yearnings, any longer.

As if a dam had burst, Kendra's lips now parted beneath his invitingly, her slender body arching eagerly to the masculine frame pressed against her, and as his grip on her wrists was slowly relinquished, her arms wrapped about him lovingly. With deliberate mastery, Rogan trailed caressing hands over her curving shape possessively, awakening within her tumultuous sensations she couldn't control, his mouth scoring a long, leisurely passage down the length of her throat to the wildly beating hollow at its base. It seemed he knew every vulnerable area in her body, making her melt to his touch, her breathing become ragged, and shocking her with the depth of the unbridled feelings coursing through her.

Emboldened by the fires of passion enveloping her, Kendra tugged his shirt loose, her slim fingers savouring the smooth warmth of the hard-contoured flesh of his heavily muscled back, the ridged planes of his broad chest, finding a vibrant pleasure in the exploration and the convulsive shudder that escaped him and had him catching her to him even more tightly.

Again Rogan's mouth claimed hers, possessing it long and deeply before seeking the curve of a bare, honey-toned shoulder, and the slipping lower as the soft cotton of her dress was pushed aside to unveil her full, swelling breasts. Kendra quivered with the intensity of her feelings as his hands proceeded to caress them slowly, tantalisingly, and then released a feverish moan when his mouth scorched a path of flame on each before closing over and lingering exquisitely about an already hardened and throbbing nipple.

With a groan, Rogan eased away from her slightly to stare down at her languorous, impassioned features with eyes still dark with desire. 'Hell! How can you possibly claim there's nothing between us after that?' he demanded thickly. 'Or is it just the challenge of the potential conquest that turns you on, sweetheart?' His gaze narrowed a little.

One particular word hit Kendra like a dash of icy water and she averted her face forlornly. 'The shoe's on the other foot, isn't it?' she countered on a choking note.

'Meaning?' A bronzed hand spanning her chin forced her glance back to his sharply.

Emotionally exhausted, she shook her head helplessly, a suspect moistness making her eyes glisten.

'You know very well what I mean!' she charged. 'It was my dislike of prospectors that was the irresistible challenge, *to you*, wasn't it?'

'Well, I certainly won't deny *you* were an irresistible challenge.' His mouth quirked with unexpected humour—to her despair.

'That's right, I suppose it amuses you to make fun of me now that you've succeeded in your aim!' she cried, beating at him with ineffectual fists.

Rogan merely imprisoned her hands within his own, and by pinioning them to the floor on either side of her head, successfully immobilised that also as he bent to possess her lips purposely once more. 'Then if I have succeeded in my aim, perhaps you wouldn't mind telling me why you're so keen to keep assaulting your future husband,' he drawled ruefully on lifting his head.

Shock held Kendra motionless for a time, hardly able to believe she had heard correctly, her eyes searching his face for some clue as to whether he was serious or not. There were traces of a smile lurking at the corners of his mouth, but it was the look in his darkly outlined eyes, deep and warm and totally devoid of mockery, that gave her the courage to put her dearest wish into words, even if somewhat hesitantly.

'Are you asking me to—to marry you?'

'Uh-uh, I'm *telling* you,' he advised drily. 'Knowing you, if I asked, you'd be bound to come up with some reason for saying no.' Framing her face with his hands, his voice grew husky as he added, 'And loving you as I do, I just can't take the chance on that happening.'

'Oh, Rogan, I adore you!' she owned fervently, able to express her own feelings at last, and twining her arms about his neck joyfully. 'There is one thing, though . . .' Her expression faltered slightly.

'I knew it!' His eyes rolled upwards expressively. 'Well, whatever it is, it doesn't make any difference! You're going to marry me, and that's that! Got it?' He eyed her mock-menacingly.

'Mmm,' she was only too ecstatic to accede. But still followed it with a lugubrious, 'Although goodness knows what everyone's going to think of me.'

'Because you're marrying a prospector, after all you've had to say about them?' he surmised, white teeth gleaming in a captivating smile.

'Well, sort of,' Kendra allowed, wrinkling her nose at him. 'I mean, for most of my life I've declared I'd never become involved with one, and then I up and marry the first wealthy one who comes along. So what does that make me?'

'Nothing more or less than what you've always been . . . a damnable threat to my self-control!' he returned in partly rueful, partly gruff tones.

Pushing herself up on one elbow, Kendra set her lips to his softly. 'I know the feeling,' she confessed deeply. 'Although *you* don't think your money's the reason I'm marrying you, do you, Rogan?' A hint of anxiety shaded her eyes as they sought his.

'Uh-uh!' His reply was reassuringly laconic. He grinned, and had her heart turning over in her chest. 'I suspected some time ago that you may not have been as indifferent as you wanted to be . . . or were determined to appear to be.'

'Yes, well, right from the beginning you made me feel so mixed up I didn't know what was happening to me,' she revealed shyly. 'Then when I did realise, I also found out who you were, and of course there wasn't anything I could do about it then.'

Rogan gazed at her incredulously. 'Are you telling me, you knew you were in love with me *before* that night Curry arrived and spilled the beans, so to speak?' And after her confirming nod, 'You little witch! That was when you were being your most sarcastic, *and* when you couldn't think of enough underhanded motives to accuse me of employing! I ought to put you over my knee for that!'

'I—well—I thought you'd probably only find it amusing if you knew, and—and at the time you were so interested in Genevieve, anyway,' she hurried to explain. 'Then when Curry arrived, I—I was just hurt I suppose at you having deceived us, and believing I'd lost any hope of—of . . .' She halted, tears starting to her eyes at the memory but which she blinked away quickly, and then shrugged. 'Well, it just seemed to all come to a head at once and I took it out on you, I guess.' She smiled sadly, appeasingly. 'I'm sorry, and especially for all those accusations I made. Although you did order me to stay out of your way too, remember. And even after I'd apologised for what I'd said.' Her glance turned slightly reproachful.

Rogan exhaled heavily, brushing her hair back from her face with a gentle hand. 'Because I was beginning to feel in dire need of a breathing space. Quite frankly, my precious, you were ripping me to shreds! By then, I wanted you more than you'll probably ever realise.'

'More than now, you mean?' she quizzed wistfully.

'God, no!' His unequivocal denial came swiftly, earnestly. 'Never more than now, my love. Nor ever more, or less, than I'll want you for the rest of my life either.' He claimed her lips in an extremely satisfying and reassuring kiss, but his eyes were starting to crinkle when he lifted his head. 'However, I can see I'm going to have to watch just exactly what I say to you in future, aren't I?'

Kendra smiled at him self-consciously. 'I think I'm

just finding it difficult to believe this is all happening really.' And sending him a chiding glance from beneath long, silky lashes, 'Especially when it was Genevieve who occupied all your time and attention.'

'My time, maybe ... my attention, rarely,' Rogan qualified in a wry drawl. 'My thoughts were usually elsewhere, with someone I would rather have been with, but who kept doing just about everything possible to avoid *my* company. I was merely playing a waiting game in the hope that the right girl just might give me some encouragement some time.'

She wished she had. It would have saved weeks of heartbreak. 'But Genevieve said ...' she began impulsively.

'Oh, yes?' Rogan inserted, brows peaking sardonically. 'And just what did Genevieve say? Something that was guaranteed to give the wrong impression, I've no doubt! She likes to think of herself as irresistible, that girl, and I don't think she was any too pleased when I made it clear right from the start that I had no intention of being manipulated into considering her as anything but a casual acquaintance.' He inclined his head enquiringly. 'So just what did Genevieve say, hmm?'

Starting to understand now why the other girl had been so malicious the night of the dance, Kendra felt she could afford to be generous in view of the way matters had worked out and gave a dismissive shake of her head.

'Oh, nothing that's of any importance any more. She was probably just out of sorts because Curry wouldn't tell her what we'd been laughing about, I expect.' Suddenly her lips began to twitch. 'Not that you looked any happier at the time, as I remember. You were positively glowering!'

'Because you'd damn well talk and laugh with him,

ut no way would you with me!' he retorted wryly.
About to continue, he surprised her by abruptly
drawing in a sharp breath, his eyes hardening to chips
of green stone. 'The bloody little bitch!' came the
explosive imprecation. 'Now it all adds up! God, why
didn't I realise before! *That's* what you were referring
to that night of the dance when you said something
about not using you to alleviate my disappointment, or
some such, and that comment this morning about my
being loath to accept her decision to marry Rex
Thorley! She told you I'd wanted to marry her, but
that she'd chosen Rex instead! That's it, isn't it,
Kendra?' He levelled a probing gaze at her.

Reluctantly, she nodded.

Rogan let loose with another epithet. 'I could choke
the troublemaking piece!' he rasped, raking a hand
through his hair savagely. 'While as for you . . .' His
anger abated to that of feigned ferocity as he returned
his attention to Kendra. 'How could you possibly
believe her? Do you really think I'm that poor a miner
that I'd settle for fool's gold when, with perhaps just a
little more patience, there was the chance I could have
the real thing?'

'Well, I wasn't to know that's how you felt, was I?'
she defended, but dimpling winsomely at the flattering
comparison. 'Perhaps if you hadn't kept accusing me
of seeing myself as Darby's keeper all the time . . .'

'That was only because I hated to see you weighed
down with so much work and responsibility,' he
disclosed deeply. 'I sometimes wondered if you
realised just how much responsibility you *did* take on
Darby's behalf, *and* how much he willingly left you
with.'

The implied criticism of her brother had her eyes
widening in surprise. 'But I thought you liked Darby.'

'And so I do—very much, as it happens. Although

that doesn't blind me to the fact that, over the years, he's had it pretty easy while you've more or less carried him.' A slow grin began playing about his firmly moulded mouth. 'Besides, would I have gone along with his matchmaking efforts if I hadn't liked him?'

'You knew?' Kendra gasped, colouring with embarrassment. 'Oh, God, I only found out about it myself after you'd left, but he said he hadn't told you!'

'Nor did he. Well, not in so many words,' Rogan amended with a laugh. 'But as you may recall, he'd had quite a bit to drink that day I met him at the hotel, and as a result he perhaps wasn't as aware of all he was saying, and *how* he was saying it, as he could have been. So taking into account the comments regarding you he had made, I had more than a fair idea of what he had in the back of his mind when he offered me that job in the store.'

'Oh, no! Then why did you accept it?'

He shrugged, smiling. 'For a couple of reasons mainly, I guess. First, because to start with I found the whole idea somewhat amusing. It was the last thing I'd ever expected to become involved with. And second, because as the evening progressed I discovered myself becoming rather more intrigued with it all. Since it was obvious Darby *was* a good bloke, as I said, I couldn't visualise him doing anybody wrong, so I decided to see for myself just what this fiery little sister of his, whom he appeared so keen to apparently match me with, was really like.'

Kendra closed her eyes in dismay at her brother's scheming, but on opening them again felt confident enough to prompt provokingly, 'And?'

'And found myself confronted with one very beautiful, but very stubborn little devil who presented a challenge I suddenly very much wanted to take up,' he owned on a husky note, his head nearing hers. 'For which, I'll never be able to thank her brother enough.'

'Nor I, for having brought home the most disturbing, not to say aggravating at times, but utterly captivating male I could ever hope to meet,' she endorsed devoutly, her lips already parting to receive his.

When they finally drew apart again, it was a long time before Kendra could regulate her breathing sufficiently to muse, 'Then your accepting the offer of work in the store had nothing at all to do with your mining operation?'

'Very little,' Rogan conceded lazily. 'It did allow me to stay in Goldfield without anyone knowing exactly who I was, or why I was there in the first place— which, in turn, did also provide me with an insight as to the locals' feelings regarding the area's potential, both past and present, plus their likely reaction to the venture—but in the main it was as a result of what Darby had had to say.' He twisted a lock of her curling hair around one of his fingers, his mouth shaping into a heart-stirring smile. 'That was, until I actually met you, of course, whereupon you promptly became my sole reason for remaining.'

A disclosure which brought a blissful glow to her deep blue eyes. 'While I had never felt quite so flustered in all my life,' she confessed with a rueful half laugh, and sent him a roguishly accusing glance from the cover of luxuriantly long lashes. 'You have such a teasing, challenging, gleam in your eyes at times, Rogan Faulkner, that it's extremely disconcerting!'

He grinned without the least sign of remorse. 'You don't do too badly at throwing down gauntlets yourself, my precious, what with all those sideswipes about prospectors.'

'I felt in distinct need of protection, and that seemed the most suitable way to keep you at a distance,' she chuckled. 'Besides, I think, subconsciously anyhow, I believed you had just too much going for you to waste your life in such a manner.'

'And now?'

She pulled a wryly amused face. 'I guess I should have known you'd turn out to be a successful miner . . . if only to prove me wrong!'

'You would rather I hadn't been?' He raised a bantering brow.

Kendra held his gaze tenderly. 'Would you believe . . . I just didn't care by then? *You* were all that mattered to me.'

Rogan gathered her to him closely. 'Mmm, I'd believe,' he granted on a deep note. 'It's always been obvious it's been the people in your life who mean most to you.' He paused. 'But now there's only one thing I want to know from you.'

'And that is?'

'When we're going to be married,' he revealed softly. 'I want you for my wife, Kendra, and as soon as it can possibly be arranged. These last weeks have been murder without you.'

As they had been for her, too, and her arms tightened about him ardently. 'How about the minute Darby and Vivian return from their honeymoon?' she suggested. 'It can't really be any sooner than that because I've promised to look after Jimmy and the store until then.' Eyeing him apologetically.

'Do you really have to?' Rogan groaned in frustration.

'I'm sorry.' She kissed him placatingly. 'But although there's plenty of others who could take care of Jimmy, and maybe even the store if it comes to that, at the same time . . .' she smiled at him in an appeal for understanding, 'I really wouldn't like to get married without Darby, and Vivian, too now, being present, if I could avoid it.'

'No, of course not,' he conceded, containing his patent disappointment. 'So how long do they expect to be away?'

'Four weeks.' She added hastily, 'Although it would take almost that long to make all the arrangements, anyway. You should know how it is with weddings and such in small towns. Everyone, but everyone, attends.' Halting, she looked at him a little anxiously. 'You were intending for us to marry in Goldfield, I take it?'

'Bride's choice, sweetheart,' he allowed indulgently.

Kendra smiled happily and went on. 'In any event, four weeks isn't such a long time. That is, unless . . .' she gazed at him doubtfully, wistfully, 'you'll be returning to Alice Springs in the meantime.'

'Uh-uh!' Rogan allayed her concern lazily, but incisively. 'As from this minute I'm taking an extended leave of absence. Curry can deal with the business, and whatever I need from home I can get our housekeeper to forward to me here, because now that I've got you, I don't mean to let you out of my sight until there's a wedding ring on your finger.'

'Not even during the nights?' she ventured to tease.

'Don't tempt me,' he partly growled, partly pleaded eloquently. 'I'm finding it difficult enough not to race you off into one of the bedrooms right now as it is!' His darkened eyes ranged the curving length of her in undisguised appreciation. 'You're unbelievably desirable, you know, and an awful threat to my self-control.'

Suddenly reminded of her dishevelled state, Kendra flushed self-consciously and would have corrected it except that a warm hand arresting hers prevented her from doing so.

'No, you look glorious just as you are,' Rogan murmured softly.

'But what if Darby should return unexpectedly?' she put forward in a voice slightly throaty with a continuing shyness.

He dismissed the idea with a shake of his head. 'I doubt he will. When I told him I was coming down here to straighten out matters between us once and for all, I suspect from the grin he gave that he'd guessed the reason why.' The revelation was drily made.

Diverted for the moment, Kendra smiled musingly. 'Which doubtlessly only added to the pleasure, and relief, your news about the Good Cheer must have afforded him. From what he was saying only this morning, I gained the impression he may have been losing some hope that you might agree to his proposal, especially in view of your enterprises always having been solely family concerns until now.'

'As they will continue to be.'

'I don't follow you.' Her eyes mirrored her puzzlement.

'Well, he is going to be my brother-in-law, isn't he?' Rogan grinned. 'And, as such, I thought my future wife would have preferred it if he was included.'

'You mean, that was the reason you decided to accept his proposal?' she gasped.

'Not entirely,' he owned honestly. 'His claim does apparently include some very high-bearing deposits of gold. As far as we can tell, he and your father were right—the reef did continue in that direction. Not that it's likely either of them would ever have discovered it, however, for according to our geologists' estimates, it appears that at some stage many aeons ago, but after the reef was originally formed, there must have been some considerable seismic activity in the region because the line of lode seems not only to have dropped some thirty feet or more, but it's now running almost at right angles to its initial course. Consequently, of course, underlie shafts never were going to be successful in re-locating it.'

Kendra nodded her comprehension, pleased for both Darby and her father's sake, though, that their supposition had been proved correct after all. None the less, there was one question she had to ask, and now she did so in amazement.

'But what if I hadn't agreed to marry you? How could you have been so certain I would?'

'Because I didn't intend to give you a minute's peace until you did,' Rogan disclosed with a smile. 'And if not today in Goldfield, then next week or next month in whatever town you moved to. As I said, I suspected you weren't as indifferent as you would have me believe, and that being so, there was no way I was going to allow you to escape me.'

'I only wish I'd never tried,' she sighed, beginning to draw his head down to hers.

A few intoxicating minutes later they reluctantly parted again on hearing a feminine voice calling from the back of the house, 'Kendra, are you there? Why isn't the store open yet?'

'Maureen,' supplied Kendra in a rueful whisper.

'If you don't answer, maybe she'll leave,' Rogan proposed hopefully in a similar undertone.

Regretfully, she had to veto the notion. 'Not Maureen. We've known each other too long and too well. She'll just come looking.'

'That could be interesting,' he drawled, drily expressive.

'Mmm, not to mention, embarrassing.' She half laughed wryly, pressing a lingering kiss to his sensuous mouth before righting her state of dress and starting to gain her feet. Once upright, and in order to forestall her friend, she called back, 'I'll be with you in a minute, Maureen!' Then watching as Rogan rose lithely to his own feet and put his shirt in place, knew she just couldn't bear to be parted from him just yet and held out an inviting hand, her eyes lifting to his in entreaty. 'Come with me?'

Clasping her fingers within his, Rogan caught her to him possessively, his lips compulsively seeking hers one last time. 'Always,' he promised huskily, and they left the room together.

Harlequin Romance

Coming Next Month

Availabe in June wherever paperback books are sold, or
through Harlequin Reader Service.

In the U.S.
901 Fuhrmann Blvd.
P.O. Box 1397
Buffalo, N.Y. 14240-1397

In Canada
P.O. Box 2800, Postal Station
5170 Yonge Street
Willowdale, Ontario M2N 6J3

Can you keep a secret?

You can keep this one plus 4 free novels

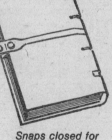

HARLEQUIN BRINGS YOU

Janet Dailey
★ AMERICANA ★

A romantic tour of America with Janet Dailey!

★

Beginning in June, enjoy this collection of your favorite previously published Janet Dailey titles, presented state by state.

Available in June wherever paperback books are sold or reserve your copy by sending your name, address and zip or postal code, along with a check or money order for $2.75 per book (plus 75¢ for postage and handling) payable to Harlequin Reader Service to:

Harlequin Reader Service

In the U.S.
901 Fuhrmann Blvd.
P.O. Box 1397
Buffalo, NY 14240

In Canada
P.O. Box 2800
Postal Station A
5170 Yonge Street
Willowdale, Ont. M2N 6J3

JDA-A-1